BAD NIGHT AT
THE CRAZY BULL

After a night of drinking at the Crazy Bull Hotel, Glen Stone wakes up to find himself in bed with a saloon girl who informs him that they have been married. When Glen returns with her to his ranch, he must deal with her refusal to do her share of the work, the assorted unsavoury characters her presence attracts, and the wrath of his long-time intended and her father. Will the arrival of horse preacher Repentance Rathbone restore harmony to the lives of the Wyoming ranchers?

JOHN DYSON

BAD NIGHT AT THE CRAZY BULL

Complete and Unabridged

LINFORD
Leicester

First published in Great Britain in 2015 by
Robert Hale Limited
London

First Linford Edition
published 2017
by arrangement with
Robert Hale
an imprint of The Crowood Press
Wiltshire

A catalogue record for this book is available
from the British Library.

ISBN 978–1–4448–3162–7

Published by
F. A. Thorpe (Publishing)
Anstey, Leicestershire

Set by Words & Graphics Ltd.
Anstey, Leicestershire
Printed and bound in Great Britain by
T. J. International Ltd., Padstow, Cornwall

This book is printed on acid-free paper

1

Glen Stone groaned when he woke from a deep sleep and held his pounding head. He was sprawled in the deep feather mattress of a big bed in the best room of the newly built Crazy Bull Hotel in the rumbustious, rootin'-tootin' cattle town of Jackson, Wyoming. Beside him was a warm-bodied half-naked young woman.

'Good morning, darling.' She propped herself up on one elbow, a hand in her dark tousled hair, which tumbled about her sharp but nonetheless attractive face.

'Who are *you*?'

'Your wife.'

'My *what*?' He sat up, startled. 'Like hell you are.'

'That ain't very polite,' she purred. 'Don't you remember?'

'Remember?' True, he seemed to recall seeing her face in the saloon

1

downstairs the previous evening. One of the dance girls, calico queens, or prairie nymphs, whatever euphemism they used for whores. 'Did I pay you to spend the night up here?'

'No,' she fluted in her southern belle twang. 'You don't have to pay me, honey. What's yours is mine. I'm your wife.'

'Cut the jokes,' he exploded. 'I'm not in the mood.'

Glen was still in his rumpled white linen day shirt, but beneath the blanket he noticed his lower parts were naked. On the floor his trousers were spread as if torn from him. That was exactly what had occurred. The gang of pranksters had carried him up, tossed him on the bed and roared with laughter as they bade him goodnight.

'Oh, God,' he groaned. 'It's all coming back.'

'You're rich, don't you remember?' She leaned over him and reached out to grab a fistful of silver and paper dollars from the adjacent dresser, giggling saucily as her bare breasts brushed his chest. 'I mean, we are rich.'

She tossed the cash in the air, laughing as it showered them. 'Two thousand dollars!'

'Aw, hell!' As if through a mirror darkly he began to remember. Glen had brought his small herd of longhorns into town, planning to run them on down to the railhead at Cheyenne. But it so happened that two big Chicago meat-packers were in Jackson to buy cows, and they wanted his. It would sure save him a long trail down to the Wyoming border, even though the cash they offered was low rate.

'Sure,' he said, sealing the deal with a handshake, and they had passed him their cheque. They had insisted he join them for a drink in the hotel bar and inveigled him into a poker game. Maybe they thought they could win back their cash.

Glen had never been a hard drinker. It clouded the judgement. Nor had he lost or won more than ten dollars before. But as the night wore on he just couldn't seem to lose. His winnings grew and grew until the two packers, like the other gamblers around the table, finally conceded defeat.

'I musta been on a lucky streak,' Glen mumbled as the pot was pushed over to him to tip into his Stetson. 'Two thou'!'

He must have guessed it was incumbent on him to buy drinks for everyone in the saloon bar, and they were a wild bunch. They had crowded around, slapping his back, toasting him, hoisting him shoulder high. More whiskeys were set up. Why not? He could afford it. Suddenly — after three years of being somewhat cold-shouldered in this township — they were all his pals. Folks loved a big winner. Like one day it might be their turn.

'I'm not used to rotgut whiskey,' he muttered gloomily to the woman. 'It musta gone to my head.'

'It certainly made you a man of

instant decisions. Surely you remember? You swept me off my feet.'

'Did I? That musta been 'fore I passed out.' But in the starkness of daylight the mist was clearing and last night's events were starting to come back to him with something of a shock. 'Aw, yeah . . .'

'They told me you were some sort of a dude, some tenderfoot from the east who had come out west to try his hand at ranching and you'd grabbed yourself some land up in the wildest, remotest spot you could find, some place called the Grand Teton, and you didn't have a clue.'

'We all have to live and learn.' He clutched his thudding brow again and muttered. 'They never did like me, those guys. I guess I got a lot more to learn.'

'Waal, honey,' she drawled, 'they said you shave your jaws once a week and bathe every month. That ain't natural in a man, not that I mind. Them smelly buzzards — '

'Buzzards? You *could* call them that. They certainly had a good cackle at my expense.'

Yes, he had been pounding round the dance floor with her like some crazy galoot. The candle-glowing, smiling faces, the barroom spinning round and round, the rough and ready men cheering, plying him with more booze. They had hoisted him and the girl up to sit on the bar. Side by side, hand in hand. A roly-poly drunk whom they called the Judge was intoning, 'Will you take this woman to be your wife?'

''I do.' That's what you said,' his companion of the bed pointed out. 'You promised to love and protect me the rest of your life. All your worldly goods on me you bestowed.'

'Oh, Jesus! So I did. But I thought it was just a game. I didn't mean it. They must have realized that.'

'Too bad, buster. You swore it in front of all them witnesses.' A nasty offended tone had come into her voice. Her face suddenly looked hard and determined.

'I'm holding you to it. We're married. You better face that fact.'

'Holy shit!' Glen sat bolt upright again. He was a well-built, handsome young man of twenty-four and his face at that moment looked as if it had been chiselled from a dark block of wood. 'What am I gonna do?'

'Do? We're gonna go back east. Buy a nice house. A fancy carriage. Spend! Spend! Spend! How about Kansas City to start? They got six-floor apartment blocks there with elevators to whisk you from the bottom to the top.'

'East? Cities? I'm sick of the east. I've seen enough of cities. No, baby, I'm headin' fifty miles north. Wyoming's the place for me.'

North! But there's nuthin' north. Only prairies and mountains and rivers and danger.'

'Yeah, that's where I live. I got a new life.' Glen glanced at her. 'You don't have to come. You can divorce me. For abandonment. For ... er ... non-consummation.' He was pretty sure

7

they hadn't *done* anything.

'Divorce you? she shrieked, rolling over him again and grabbing at the dollars. 'If I do, half of this belongs to me.'

'OK, calm down. Leave the cash alone. It's up to a judge to decide what alimony I should pay you. As I barely know you that shouldn't be much.'

'Oh, you!' She suddenly burst into tears, burying her face a little too close for comfort in his loins. 'How can you be such a brute?'

'I'm sorry.' Glen started to stroke her tangled hair, trying to soothe her. 'You must see it's impossible.'

What was she doing? To his horror he felt his manhood rise to salute her.

'No, we mustn't. It's not . . . ' But it was too late. Her fingers were fluttering. Her lips arousing him. He could not stop. Or want her to cease her ministrations. 'Aw, gee, honey,' he groaned. 'That's good.'

Then he was like a river in flood,

rolling her on to her back, taking her, gasping for breath between their kisses, sweeping onwards, his head pounding, his body throbbing. Thus their marriage was consummated, as folks say. Yes, sir, it certainly was.

There was a knock at the door and the barkeep came bustling with a tray of coffee.

'Waal, indeedy, ain't that sweet,' he drawled, 'to see you newlyweds all cuddled up. The boys sure did enjoy the party you give last night.'

'Yeah,' Glen muttered, as he disentangled himself from her and sipped at his cup. 'I bet they did. Big joke.'

'Joke? It weren't no joke. That was a real judge. Ya weddin' was all nice and legal. The Whiskey Judge they call him. He sure does like to have a laugh with the boys.'

When he had gone Glen contemplated his fate. 'By the way, miss,' he asked. 'What's your name?'

* * *

Katrina? She certainly was a good-looking woman. Well-versed in the arts of love. A high-stepper. Very astute. Some cute cookie, in fact. Maybe he could have done worse. She could have been a right slut.

Glen consoled himself with such thoughts as he harnessed his pair of horses to the wagon in the hotel livery. One minute a bachelor, the next wed. But what was done was done.

'Maybe we should give it our best try,' he said.

'What, go east?'

'No, north. Look, where I come from it's the man who makes the decisions. The wife obeys her husband. So you can either come or stay. I should warn you, it's a hard, lonesome life on my ranch.'

'Ranch?' Katrina made a face at him behind his back. 'Guess I'll tag along with you for a bit,' she muttered, more to herself.

She was certainly well-versed, too, in the arts of spending cash. She had

made him escort her to the ladies'
outfitter's store and stand about, with
his wallet handy, as she chose what she
termed her 'going-away honeymoon
outfit'. Stockings, fancy long pants, a
scarlet basque, silk nightdress and so
forth. Glen had tried to tell her she
needed more sensible garb for the
journey but she ignored him.

Now she stood there in a neat-
looking Cossack jacket, and a calf-
length flimsy skirt to show off her new
high-heeled boots. Her black hair was
swept back into a bun secured by a
scarlet ribbon. Perched on top of her
head was a silly little pillbox hat with a
spotted veil. To tell the truth she looked
real pretty in her way, but out of place
in these parts; her former profession as
a 'horizontal artiste' was written all over
her.

Glen caught her by her slim waist
and slung her up on to the wagon seat.

'Guess I'm gonna have to break you
in, Mrs Stone. You're gonna have a lot
to learn.'

'Like what?'

'You'll find out. I don't wanna spoil your honeymoon. We gotta go pick up the herd.'

'The herd? What herd?'

'My new herd of cows. I bought 'em with the money I got for my old herd of ornery longhorns. Glad to get rid of them longhorns. Most are infected with Texas fever. So I'm making a new start with a small bunch of best white-faced English Herefords. Five hundred of 'em, mostly cows and calves and a coupla breeding bulls. It's quite a challenge.'

'Just where is this so-called ranch of yours?'

'Up at Jackson Hole. Along the Snake River. God's own country. The mountains rise sheer up outa the plains. If you got any eye for beauty, Katrina, you'll love it.'

'Hmm?' She didn't sound convinced. 'Will I? So what have you done with all that cash?'

'It's in the bank where you can't get

your sticky li'l fingers on it.' Glen grunted with the effort as he heaved a couple of bags of grain up on to the wagon along with other supplies. 'We gotta go meet the boys.'

He gave the young woman the once-over again. There was something about her. She had known better times. She was not your everyday hooker. She'd got class. Something indefinable . . .

He joined her up on the box, took the reins and yelled, 'Hup!' As the two carthorses surged forwards out into Jackson's dusty main street there was a clanking and clattering from behind. He had failed to notice the cans strung from the back and the scrawled notice, JUST MARRIED!

A bunch of cowboys gave them a whooping escort. Folks turned to grin and wave as they passed. In some embarrassment Glen grinned back and was glad when he and Katrina reached the outskirts of town where Hank, Joe and Jerry were waiting with the white-faced cows. They gave shrill yips to send the beeves skedaddling across the wide plain.

'Ain't it great to be on our way?' Glen yelled, as they trundled along. 'You can take a turn to drive if you want.'

Katrina made a downturned grimace.

'Big deal.' She was not sure she was going to like being a rancher's wife.

*　★　*

The Grand Tetons rose from the plain like a craggy island from the sea. Pinnacles of sharp, snow-encrusted peaks pierced the blue sky, more than 12,000 feet high. Many folk described this scene as one of the most dramatic landscapes in all of North America. Other mountain ranges were higher and more extensive but they mostly had foothills gradually ascending towards them like stepping stones. The Tetons just exploded straight up from the level floor of Jackson Hole.

'There they are,' Glen said, reining in the wagon. 'Ain't they just an awesome sight to have on your doorstep?'

'Hmm?' Again Katrina did not sound overly impressed. 'What do they call them?'

'*Les Trois Tetons*. Three French-Canadian trappers named them that when they first saw them back in 1819. It means The Three Breasts. That's what I call my ranch. My branding-iron's shaped like three peaks.'

'The Three Tits!' Katrina gave a shrill shriek of laughter. 'Fancy callin' a damn ranch that. What do they call you? The Big Tit?'

'That's not very reverent.' Suddenly it hit Glen even more harshly that he might well be in for a heap of trouble with this woman. 'If you ain't awed by them you ain't got no soul,' he said sourly.

'Reverent? Why should I be reverent to a wall of cold mountain stone? Or to you, come to that?'

'If we're going to get along you might

show a bit of respect.'

'What, because you're my husband? All that honour-and-obey stuff is a bit outdated in my book.'

Glen let the remark pass. They had paused to allow the Herefords to water at a bend of the meandering Snake River. It was the spring of the year and the river was in tumultuous flow as the snows on the high peaks melted, feeding it with numerous tumbling streams. At this point the Snake was joined by one of its tributaries, known as Black Creek.

The young novice rancher pointed across to the triangle of land cut out by the junction and said, proudly,

'There it is. All that land over there. Right up to the mountains. That's mine.'

'So, where's the ranch house?'

'Well, it ain't exactly a house. More a cabin. But it'll be just for us. The boys have got a separate bunkhouse. It all takes time to build. It's over there, beyond them pines.'

'How many staff have you got?'

'What you mean, staff?'

'I mean a cook, maids, women to clean, sew, fetch water and do the washing. You surely don't expect me to do those sorts of things?'

'Well, yes,' Greg stuttered. 'It's generally accepted round here that the wife does her share, feeding the chickens, collecting the eggs, making the fire and keeping the stove going, that sort of thing.'

'Not me, buster,' Katrina scoffed. 'I ain't cut out for being your skivvy. Look at my hands. Soft as velvet. That's the way I intend them to stay. I've no objection to being your sex slave and companion. But that's all I aim to be.'

But — ' Glen protested.

'No buts. This is the modern age. It's 1883. So, now we're rich you better hire plenty of help for your wife. And I mean pronto.'

Glen took a deep sigh. 'I'll think about it.'

'You better had or your life ain't

gonna be worth living.'

'We've got to get the cattle across along at the ford. It'll be a rough crossing. You better hold on tight.' He urged the horses forward, bouncing the wagon down a steep slope of rough ground to where the bank of the Snake flattened out. 'Yah! Let's go.'

'Hellfire!' Katrina screamed as he cracked his bullwhip across the horses' backs and charged them into the turbulent stream which at this point was, due to the snow melt, two feet higher than it normally would have been.

'Hagh!' he yelled. The team were halfway across. 'We're gonna make it!'

Those were what could be called 'famous last words', for at that instant the wagon hit a rock and was stopped dead in its tracks with such force that Katrina was pitched tumbling head over heels into the foaming torrent.

She struggled to her feet and snatched hold of a wheel to steady her; her tiny hat was skew-whiff over one

18

ear, her hair was trailing across her face; her skimpy garments clung to her body, her powder and mascara streaked as she choked and spouted out water. And, when she regained her breath, her language was most unladylike.

'You godawful useless sonuvabitch,' she screamed. 'What you think you're playing at? You did that on purpose. You tryin' to drown me?'

'Don't be stupid. Either haul your butt back up here, or take a look underneath. Do something useful. See what's holding us.'

Katrina did as he said, groping down around the front wheel, getting another mouthful of water. 'It's stuck fast. There's a damn great boulder. What's the matter with you, you mulehead? Ain't you the sense not to run into that?' she wailed.

But his foreman Hank had seen their predicament. He had found a gnarled pole washed along in the flood and was on his horse, bringing it to their rescue.

'Here, ma'am,' he shouted. 'Hang on

to this while I hitch my hoss to t'others to give us extra pulling power.' When he had done the necessary he waded back to her. 'Maybe you better git back on board.' He politely offered her his left hand and, as she struggled in her sodden dress to make purchase, with his right palm gave her fleshy buttocks a mighty lift.

Katrina shrieked, regaining her seat in a most undignified manner as Glen shouted,

'This time do as you're told, woman. Hang on!'

Hank had grabbed the pole and was exerting all his weight to lever the boulder aside.

'Right! Now! Go.'

They were on the go again, the three horses taking the weight and trundling the wagon out on to the far bank.

'That rock didn't use to be there,' Glen said. 'It must've got rolled along in the flood.'

'Aw, shut up, you shithead. Don't make excuses now.' Katrina was trying to squeeze out her sopping dress. 'You better get me to that cabin 'fore I die of pneumonia.'

Glen would normally have helped to get the cattle across, but he left the boys to cope and headed the wagon towards a group of pines. Anything to shut her up.

Behind, the 'punchers were hooting with laughter. 'Did you see the way she took that dive?' Joe tittered. 'Arse over tit. Serve her right. Big-headed bitch.'

'Now then, boys,' Hank admonished. 'Show some respect to the boss's wife.'

'Why the hail did he git hitched to *her*?' Jerry drawled. 'He's got himself a spittin' handful, he sure has.'

★   ★   ★

That was exactly what Glen was thinking as he unlatched the cabin door and ushered Katrina in. He found kindling and split logs and soon had a fire blazing in the iron stove as Katrina struggled to divest herself of her wet garments and scraped her hair out of her eyes.

'Here,' he said, wrapping a blanket around her naked shoulders. 'You get warm. I'll go get your trunk.'

When he hefted it in she was sitting on the single bunk he had made for himself of pine wood.

'So,' she said, dolefully, looking about the sparsely furnished cabin. 'This is what you've brought me to?'

He shrugged. 'To me it's home.'

'I'll need some water boiled up to wash my hair. It's full of mud.'

'I gotta go unload the wagon and see to the horses first,' he muttered.

'That's right, don't worry 'bout me, you ill-mannered bastard.'

'What's this?' Going to light the lamp he found an erratically scrawled note on the table. *Glen, we got grizzly trouble. Come soon. Bring your gun. Abe.*

'Grizzlies?' she shrieked. 'Them great furry beasts? They kill folks, don't they?'

'Not often.'

22

'Not often? I heard they can take a man's head off with one swipe of their claws. I'm not hanging about here if them varmints are around.'

'Don't you worry. I'll go see what the trouble is in the morning. Looks like I'd better sleep in the chair tonight. There ain't room for the two of us in that cot.'

'No, there sure ain't,' she replied. 'Go on, then. Don't just stand there staring at me. Get your arse moving. I'll be needing a bathful of hot water. An' you better git some vittles cooking on the stove. I'm starving.'

'All in good time, sweetheart.'

As he left the cabin he reflected that he had been at Jackson Hole for three hard but satisfying years. He could be proud of what he had achieved. Only a few days ago the world had seemed hunky-dory. But now a cloud of gloom hung over him. Yes, he was in deep trouble. But his biggest problem would be tomorrow when he visited his nearest neighbour, Abe Cousins, who had a ranch fifteen miles upriver. How could he explain about Katrina? What would he say to Abe's sweet, sixteen-year-old daughter, Susan, the girl who was plainly expecting to be his wife?

2

Seven men hanging from the crossbeam of a barn door on one of Cheyenne's dusty streets had been a stark introduction to the west for Glen Stone. He had travelled to that godforsaken spot in the comfort of a Central Pacific Pullman, clicketing along at eighteen miles an hour, double doors and windows maintaining an even temperature of 70° Fahrenheit or whatever it was outside. Stewards attended to his needs. There was fine food, newspapers and novels for sale. Excellent sleeping berths. All the comforts of civilization as they crossed the wide prairies, heading towards the Rockies.

Then, in his city suit, carpetbag in hand, he had climbed down from the Pullman into another world. Out of the east into the west. He had watched the great train go rattling away, pumping a column of smoke into the heavens, and had pushed through a motley crowd, past unpainted clapboard stores and houses, peering into a pandemonium of gaming houses and saloons filled with desperate-looking characters. Then he had been struck by the sight of the corpses dangling.

That had been three years ago, the day he had met Hank Jones. The older man was leaning on a corral rail, mournfully contemplating his herd of fifty cows, bulls and calves.

'What?' Glen pointed to the dead men. 'Why?'

'Vigilantes,' Hank said. 'They've strung up hundreds of ruffians the past few months. Good job, too.'

'Are those your cows, mister?'

'They sure are. Why, you wanna buy them? A hundred dollars the bunch to you, son.'

'Well, I would if I had any land to put them on. How would I go about buying a small ranch around here?'

'Are you joking?'

26

'No, why? That's my ambition. I heard this was good cattle country.'

'Yeah, it is. You see them dreary plains stretching away for hundreds of miles to the west? Once the Indians were gone, and most of the vast buffalo herds, too, a few white settlers grabbed the land. There's ranches out there now running thirty-five thousand head of stock. And you know what? They defend it with their guns. They don't like newcomers, or 'nesters' as they call 'em, trying to move in.'

'Well, there must be some land somewhere.'

Maybe there is a piece would be ideal for a beginner like you. I've druv this small herd four hundred miles all the way down here to sell. My plan is to get outa this wilderness, go back to civilization.'

'Really? Who are all these people? Where are they heading to?'

'The Black Hills. Deadwood City. They think they'll strike gold, git rich. Maybe that's your better option, pal.'

'I dunno,' Glen had muttered. 'I ain't sure what to do. What are all those big six-horse wagons being loaded up with freight?'

'That's what they are: freighters. They'll be travelling out hundreds of miles to the far-flung settlements. All the necessities of life and a few of the luxuries, too.'

'I'd really like to have a ranch. I've got a bit of cash. Maybe if I bought you a beer you could give me a few pointers, mister. I'm not familiar yet with Wyoming Territory.'

'I'll take you up on that offer, seeing as how I'm broke.'

They had headed for the saloon where the lanky old 'puncher told him his sad story.

'My wife's dead of the smallpox. My herd of five hundred head was run off by rustlers who burned my cabin to the ground. There's some real bad sorts roaming hereabouts: deadbeats, convicts, killers, taking what they want. If I was you, son, I'd git back on that train and go home.'

'Aw, you've had bad luck. It can't be *all* that bad,' Glen said, calling for beers, trying to cheer the man up. 'Where's the best place for me to go to find some land?'

It had taken more than one beer to elicit much information out of the man. But Hank suddenly had a change of heart.

'Hot damn,' he cried. 'You're a real greenhorn, aintcha. A hundred greenbacks for the herd, thirty in advance as a month's wages to me an' I'll show you just where you can start. We'll drive these cows all the way back to where we come from.'

So it happened that Glen found himself riding a ten-dollar horse, a fifteen-dollar Colt .45 tucked in his belt, learning how to trail cattle up through Laramie and Medicine Bow on a four-hundred-mile journey through the Absoroka range to the north and the Wind River mountains until they reached Jackson Hole.

'There y'are, young feller. That piece of land across the river. Once it was mine. Now it's yourn.'

'You planning to stay and be my foreman, Hank?' Glen had asked.

'Your ramrodder? Waal, I ain't got no wish to be the boss man no more. Sure, I'll stay, if that's what you want. We'll be needing a coupla more hands. I know just the boys. Hey, look at them cattle gittin' frisky. Seems like they're glad to be home.'

★   ★   ★

Yes, that was three years ago. He and Hank had worked hard, felling lodge-pole pines to build a new cabin, adding a bunkhouse, stabling, outhouses and corrals. Glen had used the carpentry skills he had learned in his father's furniture factory back in Springfield, Ohio.

Just to make things legal he had paid Hank another fifty dollars and they visited an attorney's office in Jackson to draw up the deeds. As was the rough and ready custom he put an advertisement in the *Jackson Times* that he was the new owner. It let folks know who was who and what was what.

Glen had been wary of a repeat visit by rustlers for a while and carried a rifle and sidearm wherever he rode. Eventually he decided it must have been a one-off, for life in the glorious setting along the Snake valley proved to be fine and peaceful. He was proud to be owner of the Trois Tetons ranch.

Of course, no income came in during those three years, but Glen had lived frugally, spending his patrimony carefully. He had been the youngest of three brothers. The eldest, James, was a bit of a goody-goody, the apple of his father's eye, and he had more or less taken over the running of the factory. The middle one, Caleb, was a different kettle of fish, a handsome skirt-chaser, with little taste for hard graft. He was more interested in frequenting saloons and gambling hells. Glen, too, had little interest in spending his life in the factory, supervising the workers at their lathes all day. He had been put to military college for two years, had learned to ride and handle arms, but decided the parade-ground pomp was not for him. His father despaired of them both but gave each a lump sum of $2,000 and told them to do as they could with it. 'You might as well have it now as when I'm dead,' he said.

The money had been a godsend, had seen Glen through those three years. He survived blizzards that wiped out other ranchers. He bought some of their beeves, increased his stock, and early that spring they had rounded up the half-wild longhorns, rousting them out of coulées and canyons beneath the great rock wall of mountains. The calves had grown, the herd had multiplied. Glen was surprised to find he had a thousand head.

'I couldn't have done this without Hank's wise advice,' he told Susan Cousins. 'I learned everything from

him. That old guy's a walking encyclo-
paedia of cattle lore. We're heading the
herd for market tomorrow. Wish me
luck.'

The offer of six dollars a head from
the two cattle buyers at Jackson was less
than he might have got in Cheyenne,
but when he added it up $6,000 was
more than his wildest expectations.
Suddenly he was a wealthy man with
cash in the bank. No wonder he felt like
celebrating that night. Now he could
afford to get wed, start a family. He
must have been in a joyful mood when
he accepted the packers' invitation to
join them in the poker game.

'If only I'd never met them, had
trailed on to Cheyenne,' he muttered
outside the cabin the next morning as,
in the dawn light, he faced his new
situation. He warmed his saddle horse
Crackers's bit before easing it into the
animal's mouth. 'I'd have been on top
of the world.'

The pinto nudged him, trying to
poke his nose into his topcoat pocket.

'Yeah, it's OK for you, old pal. All you want is a cracker, doncha? Here y'are.' His horse had a terrible fondness for hardtack biscuits.

'What's done is done,' he sighed, as he swung aboard. 'An' it don't look like it can be undone.'

He didn't wake Katrina, whom he had left sleeping in his bunk. 'So long,' he called to the men. 'I'm off to meet a bear.'

'Take care,' Hank warned.

Glen rode straight-backed, military style, tugging his flat-crowned Stetson over his brow, for it was early in the year and a chill wind was whistling down from the still snow-covered slopes of the Yellowstone Park, which rose high to the far north. It contained a volcanic crater, lying dormant, as its hot gushing springs showed, and in 1872 had become the USA's first national park and wildlife refuge. That was probably where the grizzly had come from, waking from its winter sleep in its den and feeling real mean and hungry.

In his saddle boot was his Winchester rifle, brought out in '81, an improvement on the 1873 model, stronger and simpler with a steel frame and butt plate and a sliding lid to keep out dirt and snow.

'Oh, God!' He was riding into Abraham Cousins's ranch when it suddenly occurred to him: he needed more bullets in the magazine.

Abe had come out to greet him. Glen made a gesture of despair.

'What a fool I am. I forgot to stock up on boxes of shells t'other morning in Jackson. That woman put me in such a tizz.'

'What woman?'

'My wife — I gone and got married, Abe.'

'You *what?*' Cousins stared at him almost with disbelief. 'You got wed? Why? What for? What's Susan going to say?'

'That's what I'm worried about. Where is she?'

'She's out for her mornin' ride.'

'Right. Let's get this over with first. What's all this about a grizzly?'

'He's taken one of our horses. It's lying dead and mauled along in the canyon. Once a grizzly gets a taste for horsemeat he'll do it again. He's gotta be put down. I'd do it but, you know . . . '

Glen, still on horseback, nodded. Abe suffered from a palsied hand. He was no alcoholic: it was some odd disease. He couldn't even pour coffee from the pot without shaking it all over everyone.

'None of the boys are hot shots. But if you ain't got the .44 shells we'd better call it off. We only got .45s.'

'No, I'll give it a try.' To tell the truth he was so upset about facing Susan he didn't much care whether he lived or died. 'Let's go.'

Several of Abe's 'punchers accompanied them along to where the dead horse lay. Black crows were pecking at its innards and rose up with harsh caws, flapping off as they approached. The bloody meat was out in the open on a grassy knoll. A grizzly going at thirty miles an hour downhill with the advantage of surprise could catch a horse and drag it down. This one hadn't had much chance.

'We'll just have to wait for him to arrive,' Glen said, stepping down. 'Can one of you hold on to Crackers for me?'

He levered a shell into the breech of the Winchester and rested the barrel on a rock as he lay down. The men knelt behind him, watching with interest. They didn't have long to wait.

'Christ! There he is,' one hissed.

A huge grizzly had suddenly appeared out of the forest, his humped back reveal-ing his massive strength. He loomed, peering, nostrils quivering, from a rise up above them. He showed no fear. If he came from the Yellowstone he had probably never been hunted before. Glen's mouth had gone very dry.

'Whoo! He's a big one.'

'Yeah,' another man said. 'I never seen one like him.'

'How many slugs you got?' Abe asked.

'Two. If I miss with the first I'll have a coupla seconds to get him with the next — '

'Two?'

There was a rustling from behind and, glancing round, Glen saw that all of the boys had taken to their heels, running to shin up pine trees or get back to their hitched horses to scramble into the saddles. Even Abe was backing away.

'Leave it, Glen, don't be a fool.'

But it was too late for that. The grizzly was hurtling down the slope towards him, obviously angered that anyone should be near his breakfast. Glen squinted along the sights, awaited his chance, then fired. He was sure he had hit him but the bear roared with pain and kept coming. Glen instinctively jumped back on to his boot heels, but it was no good running. He levered the Winchester, stood his ground and fired again. The grizzly gave another agonized roar and leapt for him, claws extended, his slavering jaws and teeth open wide. He slithered along the grass, tumbled over a boulder and lay dead at Glen's feet.

When the men climbed down from their trees, somewhat shamefaced, Glen took a deep breath and forced a grin.

'Nuthin' to it,' he said.

'Look at the fangs on him.' Abe had rejoined him. 'Thanks, Glen. You want the pelt? It's yourn. Make a nice bedcover in the winter for you and your new wife.'

'No, I don't think so.' Glen had seen a girl on a feisty young filly racing over the hillside towards them and he felt more scared now than when he had seen the grizzly. 'Aw, gee. What am I gonna say?'

Susan Cousins, in faded tight blue jeans 'de Nîmes', a blouse and buckskin coat, rode astride like a cowboy, her blonde curls like a halo in the early sunrise. Her face was flushed as she pulled in the three-year-old and smiled at Glen.

'You got him? Well done. You mighta told me, Dad.'

'It's men's work,' her father replied. 'Dangerous. In my opinion Glen's damn lucky to be alive. Got him with the second shot.'

Glen's heart began pounding faster than it usually did when he saw Susan. She looked so radiant in the morning sunlight, her blue eyes wide and sparkling, her teeth so white, her pretty little retroussé nose wrinkling as she laughed.

'I knew you could do it, Glen.' She slipped from the saddle, and as she squeezed his arm he could feel the warm press of her breast through her blouse. 'Are you gonna stay all day?'

In the past he would have done, but young Stone's heart sank, as they say, like a stone, and he forced himself to step away. The boys were making a travois of branches on which to load the grizzly. 'Can you . . . ?' He swallowed hard, trying to get the words out. 'Susan, can I speak to you?'

'Susan?' She smiled, surprised. 'Why so formal? Why not Sue? How did you get on in Jackson?'

He moved away from the men so that they could not be heard. 'I got to tell you . . .'

'Come on, cough it out. What?'

'I'm wed.'

The girl recoiled as if struck in the face.

'You what?'

His words came out in a hurried jumble. 'I was terrible drunk. I got married. I didn't mean to. I thought it was a joke. But it's real. A nightmare. I'm sorry. I really am. I wanted you.'

'Stop. Let's get this straight. You're wed. Who to?'

'A prostitute. Well, she was. She won't be no more. Katrina. She's not a bad woman. A bit sharp. She's back at the cabin.'

'You're telling me you got drunk, you met a whore and you went to bed with her? When you had more or less promised me?'

'No, I didn't know. I woke up and there she was in bed.'

'To think I trusted you. I was keeping myself for you.' She blinked back tears. 'Why, when you found this woman in your bed, didn't you just tell her to clear out?'

'I shoulda done.'

'So, what did you do? No, don't tell me.'

He nodded, like a naughty boy before the headmistress. 'I guess I got carried away.'

'You disgust me.' Susan turned, leapt into the saddle of the filly and went racing away towards the mountainside.

Glen glanced at Abe, climbed on to Crackers and went pounding after her. He couldn't just leave like this. He had to explain. But Crackers was no race-horse. Susan was riding over the slope of the hill, disappearing out of his life. He topped the ridge and rode on. Eventually he saw her standing by a knot of pines, her head pressed into her horse's neck, quietly sobbing.

'Go away,' she screamed, her face distraught. 'I never want to see you again. You deceived me.'

'Susan.' He tried gently to soothe her shaking back. 'I love you.'

'How can you say that? What are you, some Mormon? Do you want *two* wives? I've had other men I liked asking to marry me, but I — ' She broke down sobbing, her pretty face agonized, fisting away the tears. 'Go,' she screamed. 'Go back to your whore. Don't ever come near me again.'

'I can't just — will you be OK?'

'Yes, I need to be alone. Just go.'

As he rode back down the trail Glen felt like he had been banished from paradise and was entering purgatory. The Trois Tetons no longer seemed like home, sweet home.

3

Sometimes it seemed like trouble was Zane Hollister's middle name. There had been trouble up in the cold grey canyons of Montana when they tried to ambush a consignment of gold. The double-barrelled shotguns of the six heavily armed guards blew young Curly and the black guy Moses to smithereens with their first volley. Zane had killed one of the guards but, as lead flew, he made a hasty withdrawal before the vigilantes got on their trail.

There had been more trouble at Missoula when one of the Mexicans, or probably all three, raped that young girl. Zane had never fancied a hempen necktie and folks could get pretty riled up about that sort of fool thing. They had headed out of town fast, following the Bitteroot River down to Idaho Territory.

Now there were nine of them: his long-time pal, the blond, blue-eyed Kenny Hayward — they had shared a cell in the penitentiary; the three greasers and four others, as hard a bunch of desperadoes as any lone traveller could wish not to meet. And they were looking for more prey.

They rode hard for a couple of hundred miles, heading through the Little Lost Pass between the Lemhi and Lost River hills, on beneath Saddle Mountain and across the Snake River plain. The new grass was greening over and their horses were still in good condition, for at nights they hobbled their forefeet so they could hop about and graze without going far.

Idaho Falls was just a cluster of new-planed clap-board cabins huddled around a granary, a butcher's shop and a couple of other stores which served the far-flung ranches.

'Howdy y'all,' Zane called, as he pushed through the batwing doors of a saloon which had *Welcome Stranger*

45

scrawled on its false-front in blood-red paint. A bunch of cowpokes playing cards at the far end looked along. Their runty ponies were hitched outside. Most travellers went hung with iron in these parts, so they paid little heed.

'Set 'em up,' Zane told the barkeep. 'Whiskey for me an' my boys.'

'Yes, sir.' The poky-nosed, skinny creep of a 'keep eyed, nervously, the scurvy bunch of desperadoes who had trailed in behind Zane. He turned the spigot of a barrel and filled clay tumblers with the fiery corn mash. 'There y'are, gents.'

'Them sure are some mountains over yonder to the east. How do they call 'em?'

'That's the Teton range, sir.'

'Would I be right in thinking there's a way through into Wyoming?'

'Yes, sir. Just follow the Snake through the gorge and it'll lead you up to Jackson.'

'Jackson? That sounds int'restin'.' Zane raised his mug and grinned at his little sidekick, Kenny. 'We were there about three years ago, weren't we? Musta come full circle.'

Kenny looked like a banty little boxer, his nose broken and flattened hard into his face with just a fleshy turned-up snub. He wore filthy, once-red long johns and trousers suspended by a bit of rope, a battered hat on his head, a gunbelt slung round his loins.

He grinned gappy teeth and drawled, 'Thought I recognized them three peaks. Musta seen 'em from t'other side.' He tittered as he slurped his whiskey. 'That sure was a night to remember.'

'The less said about that night the better.' Zane jerked his jaw back in an angry grimace, lowering his voice. 'You disobeyed my orders, Kenny. There was no need to slit that good lady's throat. She must have been all of fifty. I can't see what attracts you to such wrinkly creatures.'

'Aw, I ain't averse to a few wrinkles. Fourteen to ninety's fair game for me.'

Kenny's pale-blue eyes stared maniacally as he cackled. 'That old sow shouldn't've said what she did to me. It weren't nice. Bet her old man musta got a shock when he got back. No cabin, no herd, no wife. Anyway, you said 'no witnesses'. In my book that includes wimmin, too.'

Zane Hollister was six feet tall and lean from years of hard riding. In his wide-brimmed hat, black bandanna, red shirt, chaps and stout boots he stood and sampled the brew. His was a savage countenance: frowning dark eyes and hooked nose amid unruly black hair and beard. He gave a jerk of his head and beckoned Kenny away from his noisy *compadres*, who were whooping up the whiskey.

'Look,' he growled, 'you kill or rape any more women they're bound to hound us down. You gotta change your ways, boy.'

'Don't call me boy,' Kenny spat back. 'I ain't ya boy any more.'

The older man grimaced, tightening

his jaw. 'Calm down. We gotta change our style. I'm getting tired of running, Kenny. What have we got for it all? Nothing. We ain't gittin' no younger nor richer. You can go your way if you want. But I'm thinkin' of settling down.'

'Settlin' down? That's a joke.'

'I'm plannin' on gittin' myself a saloon. Not like this dump. A real one where I can just sit and see the cash flow in from the fools on t'other side of the bar.'

'A saloon?' Kenny curled his lip. 'How can *you* git a saloon?'

'You build one. Or buy one. That's what you do.'

'Oh, yeah,' Kenny scoffed. 'Your last big idea didn't work so well, did it? We'll dig a mine and git rich up at Last Chance Gulch, Montana. Huh!'

'How did I know the big boys had taken over? They didn't leave much for us small fry. We made a living, didn't we?' A faraway look came into Zane's eyes as he thought of the Gulch, now named Helena, the scene of a big scramble for riches in the sixties. By '68 16 million dollars in gold had been taken out. 'They reckon a man was kilt every day there in the old days. It musta been some crazy town.'

'Well, it ain't no more.' Kenny recalled Helena as they had found it. Cold, grey, respectable. A town of neat pitched-roof cabins. A company town. 'Dunno how I stuck it fer a year.'

There was a commotion going on in the corner, where the Mexicans had found a dusty, worn roulette table. Raoul, in his big sombrero and tattered leather breeches, vicious spurs jangling, screeched, 'Ayaiee, meester! You got the leetle ball for thees table?'

'No,' the 'keep whined, wishing they'd all be on their way. 'We don't use it no more.'

'How about zee señorita?' Raoul flashed gold teeth. 'The preety dancin' girl you got upstair?'

'No, only my old mother's up there.'

'She'll do.' Kenny grinned.

'That's enough,' Zane hollered. 'That's all the whiskey we'll have. We'll be movin' outa here pronto. Keep ya wits about you. We got a long ride.'

There was a board on the back shelf, chalk-scrawled: PIGS' TROTTERS 50C, HAMBURGERS, 50C. Zane slapped four silver dollars on the bar. 'Give 'em hamburgers, pal. Is there a bank in this town?'

'Yes, sir. Just along the street.'

'Good, I need to make a withdrawal.' He nudged Kenny. 'You boys wait here. We won't be long.'

'How about a sheriff?' Kenny asked. 'You got one of them?'

'No, sir,' the 'keep stuttered. 'I mean, yes, sir. He's outa town.'

'Aw, what a shame. I wanted to make his acquaintance.'

The other men hung along the bar in their scruffy range clothes — Billy Bob Creed, Jake Simms, Zoot Evans and Nelson Chines — grinned. 'Us, too.'

'Just one other thing,' Zane said to the barman. 'You want to sell that roulette table? I'll pay twenty dollars.'

'Well, I dunno.' The 'keep tested with his teeth the golden eagle that Zane slapped down. 'Yes, OK, it's yourn.'

That made the men cackle even more until Zane snapped, 'Billy Bob, Zoot, load it on a bronc. Rope it tight, that's a precious commodity. I'm gonna open a bar.'

As he and Kenny ambled across to the bank Zane growled, 'We'll do this quiet, like.'

There was hardly a soul around. It was a Monday and most of the stores were still closed; just a few men were hoisting sacks over at the grain store.

Nobody in the bank, either.

'Good mornin', sir,' Zane greeted the clerk behind his iron grille. 'Is the manager in?'

'I *am* the manager,' the greyhair in his celluloid collar replied. 'Can I help you gentlemen?'

'You surely can, sir. I wish to cash this cheque.' Zane fluttered it temptingly through the archway in the grille but, as the manager reached to take it, Zane caught hold of his wrist in an iron grip and hauled the man hard forward to smash his face up against the iron bars. 'Hand over the keys to the safe and you stay healthy.'

The manager's eyes bulged, his face was squashed out of shape. With his free hand he scrambled to find the bunch of keys in a drawer. He offered them, pleadingly.

'Take them.'

'Thank you, sir.' Zane grabbed the man's other wrist and pulled both arms out as Kenny stepped forward and stuck a stiletto into his jugular. 'Dear, dear, what a lot of blood!'

He picked up the keys, opened a door and led the way into the back office.

'I do declare, what a fine old safe. This would have taken a bit of busting, Kenny.'

But Kenny was making sure the manager was dead and relieving him of his gold watch and taking any bills that were in the cash drawers, stuffing them into a gunny sack.

'Christ!' Zane shrilled. 'We've hit the jackpot.'

He was pulling out bags of coins and stacks of greenbacks from the shelves of the unlocked safe. 'Stick it in your bag. We'll count up when we're outa here.'

'Why not count up now? We don't have to share all this with them other dumb hicks.'

'Quite so. Why not? There don't seem to be no other customers.'

The two men began greedily thumbing through the notes.

'Hell's bells, there's more'n six thou here.'

'And about a thousand in gold coin in the bags.'

'I'll stick the notes in the sack for us. Or for our saloon. And one of the bags of coin. Looks like five hundred dollars in t'other. We'll give that to the boys.'

'Yeah, we don't want to spile 'em, do we?' Kenny grinned. 'They'd only spend it on whiskey and whores.'

'Oh, my God!' a voice exclaimed.

Zane and Kenny froze. When they peered through the crack of the door they could see a woman in a sun bonnet and a coarse dress staring through the grille at the manager in his pool of blood. She was opening her mouth to scream when Kenny's throwing knife thudded into her chest. She toppled back against the wall and slid to the floor, her mouth still wide open. Kenny knelt over her.

'Wrong time, wrong place, lady,' he said, twisting the blade. He pulled it out, then stuck it in her again and again until she was dead.

'Come on! Move!' Zane urged. 'Leave her.'

Outside all was quiet. As they hurried back along the sidewalk Kenny used his knife to cut free from the hitching rails any horses he saw, waving them away to go skittering off down the street. He hung on to a couple of good ones.

Zane swung the gunny sack over his shoulder to hang it from his saddle horn.

'I reckon some rancher must have sold his herd an' paid it into the bank yesterday,' he surmised. 'The problem is, what to do with them guys in the saloon? They know our faces.'

'No witnesses,' Kenny replied, drawing his long-barrelled Lefaucheu .45 to hold it behind his back.

'What's goin' on?' the 'keep quavered as they burst back into the saloon.

'Come on, boys. Look smart. This is for you.' Zane tossed the bag of coin at Billy Bob. 'And this for you.' He pulled out his southern-made Rigdon & Ansley six-shooter and sent the 'keep spinning back to crash on to his barrel, a bullet in his guts. 'Kill 'em all,' he screamed.

The card players were scrambling to their feet, snatching out their cheap six-guns. One was fast.

'Agh!' Nelson groaned as a bullet lodged in his side.

Raoul was faster and the cow-puncher, too, went tumbling as bullets whined and ricocheted about the saloon. Acrid gunsmoke curled over all the dead card players as the boys held their fire. Suddenly there was silence.

'That sure spoiled their game,' Jake growled, thumbing his hammer, ready for any more who came.

On the floor Nelson clutched his insides and begged, 'Boys, take me with you. I can ride.'

Zane nodded at Jake, who put a bullet through Nelson's head. There were shouts from along the street.

'Sorry, Nelson,' Jake muttered. 'It's best. You couldn't have lasted long.'

'That's the way it is,' Zane yelled. 'Come on, let's get outa here.' But first' — he went over to the till — 'I'll have my golden eagle back.'

The gang ran out of the saloon, sending bullets whistling and caroming towards a straggle of men and women who were running towards them. They soon changed course and dashed for cover. Kenny grinned up at the *Welcome Stranger* sign.

'They'll have to change the name of this place when we're gone.' He fired his French-made pistol at it and set his mustang haring away.

The Mexicans were wheeling their mustangs, sending more lead flying as the gang galloped off across the plain.

'Let's give these gringo chickens a taste of lead,' Raoul cried, spurring his stallion and charging down the dirt street, firing wildly at all and sundry. His *compañeros* joined in, howling with glee, as their bullets shattered windows and splintered doors.

'*Viva* Mexico,' Raoul shouted, spending his last slug.

'OK, boys. *Andale*. Let's go.' They chased after their departing comrades.

4

Glen Stone watched as the eastern sky was flushed crimson as the sun's rays flickered across the horizon and a new day dawned. He had left the cabin in darkness, quietly saddled Crackers and, in the rarefied air at 6,000 feet, still lit by moon and stars, he headed away through rocks and pines across his range.

Some desperate instinct had drawn him ten miles north to a string of lakes, making his way along the shorelines, skirting the dense, dark forest until he reached a promontory and took his stand on 'our rock' as they had named it.

Suddenly the placid lake turned a brilliant orange as the sun's rays caught it and, in its still surface, the mountains were perfectly mirrored in a deep rich blue. Behind him the peaks of the Trois

Tetons were intercut by the deep purples of the canyons, their higher slopes of snow now the colour of a pink rose. In the past he and Susan had often met here to be at one in these magical mornings of early summer. An absurd hope made him long for her to be there, although he knew she wouldn't, couldn't be. The realization of this made him want to howl like a lonesome wolf.

He had left Katrina asleep in the bunk, slipped from his blankets on the hard floorboards and gone out to breathe in the sharp clarity of the morning air.

For weeks she had been nagging him to take her into Jackson to collect the new bed she had sent for from the mail order catalogue. Glen had made his excuses that he was too busy with the other men, building a timber extension to the cabin, and there was no point in fetching it until the new bedroom was ready. But now the work was done and he had agreed. Today was the appointed day.

When he had helped Hank drive those first, half-wild, unruly longhorns the 400 miles back from Cheyenne across the plains, sitting in the saddle all day, learning the tricks of the cowboy's trade, sleeping by a campfire under the stars, and reached Jackson Hole he had known that this was the place he wanted to be. Now he was not so sure.

As Crackers craned to reach a thistle on the mountainside Glen watched trumpeter swans, newly arrived from the south, gliding in to ripple the lake's glassy surface, and a moose, probing the water's edge for weed. The moose had shed his great rack of antlers and would grow a fine new set ready for the annual rut: males fighting for dominance, for females. In the animal — and human — world that basic urge was everywhere.

For thousands of years these forests and lakes had teemed with these creatures but since the arrival of the mountain men in the 1820s they had been so reduced that few trappers were now seen in the Hole. That was their word for a valley like this amid the mountains.

'Come on, boy,' he called to Crackers. He swung back into the saddle. 'Let's go home. This is a fool's errand.'

He took one last look at the Cousins's spread across the far side of the lake, its grasses illumined like gold in the early sunlight. What if they did meet? What could he offer her? All hope of having a life together was over. Why couldn't he accept that?

A bighorn ram, with his peculiar twirled horns, had come from the far side of the steep mountain face, but instead of showing any fear he trotted towards them. Glen reached for his rifle. This fellow would taste good on a dinner plate. But he paused, as curious about the ram as the ram was about them.

'Hey, boy.' Glen clicked his fingers at him, trying to coax him closer. After a brief inspection the ram had seen enough, and hurried away, his huge testicles swaying, bounding up the cliff rocks in search, no doubt, of his harem.

'You wanna be more careful,' Glen shouted. 'Us humans ain't all as friendly as me.'

The beavers had suffered most in the recent past, slaughtered almost to extinction for their fur. Retracing his trail along the lake edge to the estuary of a stream he reined in again when he saw one busy outside his lodge. This one raised himself like a tubby, toothy old man, whiskers flickering, to see who this new arrival could be.

It was good to see them making a comeback even though they were still being trapped. Again with a pang of regret he remembered how Susan and he had loved to watch them. There would be no hope of sharing such moments with Katrina. She liked to lie abed of morns and screeched with horror at the thought of getting up on to a horse. 'You won't get me on one of those brutes,' she told him.

He inspected the new short-horned Herefords as he rode back across their scrubby range. They were settling in well and barely bothered to skitter out of his path.

'They ain't half as troublesome as them durn vicious longhorns,' he remarked to Crackers. Well, at least unlike Katrina, the horse didn't answer back.

'Where've you been?' were her aggrieved words when he got back. 'Out mooning over your lost love?'

Somebody must have filled her in about his former infatuation with the rancher's daughter fifteen miles away.

'I had to cook my own breakfast. You trying to get out of going to Jackson? We oughta make an early start.' An odd remark, as she was still in her nightgown, her dark hair filled with curler rags hanging down about her white face. A cigarette dangled from her lips, the smoke spiralling as she studied the mail order catalogue. 'There's some more stuff here we need to get.'

'I doubt it,' Glen muttered. 'What's the use of all that junk?'

'You miserable tightwad, what's the matter with you? First stop in Jackson is the bank. You get some of that moolah out. I'm planning to have a good time. What's the point in having all that cash if you don't spend it?'

In vain Glen tried to point out that he had to abide by a business plan. The cash from his gambling win and for the longhorns had to be dipped into with care over the next two or three years, until the Herefords were ready for market. He needed to keep enough back to pay the men's wages, various demands, household expenses . . .

'Household expenses!' she snorted with exasperation. 'You call this a household?'

'Here,' he said, tossing a bloody-headed jack-rabbit on to the table. 'Tomorrow's supper. If we ain't back by then the boys can have it. But I'm telling you, Katrina, I ain't staying long in Jackson. I got a ranch to run.'

'Eugh!' She grimaced, flicking her fingers at the dead animal. 'Take it away. What am I s'posed to do with it?'

'Well, it would be nice if you could make a pastry crust, or even some biscuits.'

He didn't wait for a reply but went outside, skinned and gutted the rabbit, chopped it into manageable chunks and tossed the offal into a bonfire to avoid attracting bears. He filled an iron cauldron with water and chucked the meat in, hanging it over the fire to boil.

'Open a can of tomatoes, see what else you can find for flavour,' he said to young Joe. 'Let it simmer and give it a stir now and again.' Maybe, he thought, it *was* time to hire themselves a cook.

When he had the wagon horses in the traces and ready to go, he found a couple of warm eggs under one of the hens in their coop and rustled himself up some breakfast. Katrina was pouting into a mirror, prettifying herself and rougeing her lips and cheeks.

'Won't it be great to have our own bed at last, honey.' She permitted him an intimate, knowing smile. 'I cain't wait.'

Glen nodded, his mouth full of omelette. He certainly was getting tired of sleeping on the floor. He had to admit that her razor-sharp body brought him alive. And Katrina was always as eager as he was. There was nothing wrong with their relationship in that way. In fact, his new wife had shocked him by doing things he had never dreamed a woman would do with a man. Pleasantly shocking, he had to admit. The only trouble was, once started she wanted to go on and on. After a a hard day's work Glen needed his sleep. But a man could hardly complain about being made love to.

Nor was he now worried about catching a disease 'tween the legs. Katrina had assured him the doc had given her a clean bill of health only recently. She also informed him that, due to a botched abortion, the medics had told her she could not have a child.

'That don't worry me,' she said. 'Who wants to be wiping the bottoms of some screaming little bastards, anyhow?'

In some ways that was a relief. Glen did not fancy fathering a child by her. So why not just have some guilt-free fun times? Sometimes, however, all the activity left him with a feeling of futility. He would have loved to bring up a couple of kids by 'the right girl'. Oh, no, not *her* again!

'Come on,' he growled. 'I got the wagon ready. It's a long trek to Jackson, near on fifty miles, but we should be able to make it 'fore sundown.'

$$\star \quad \star \quad \star$$

Zane and his men had holed up in Death Canyon, a dark, forbidding place beneath Buck Mountain, which soared to 12,000 feet above them.

'We gotta split up,' he said. 'Me an' Kenny an' Billy Bob are going into

Jackson. You boys gotta stay put, lie low for a few more days.'

'That ain't fair,' Zoot Evans whined. 'Why should y'all have the fun?'

'Yuh.' Jake Simms had a hundred dollars burning a hole in his pocket. 'I got me a terrible thirst, Zane. Why cain't we come?'

'That's right.' Zoot giggled. 'An' I got me a terrible hankering to tickle them li'l gaudy-gals in that Jackson saloon.'

'Thees canyon geev me the creeps,' Raoul cried. 'Eet go nowhere. The sides like walls. Death Canyon? They call it good. Ees deathtrap, that what it ees. Why the hell we got to stay here?'

'Because, you dumbclucks, we all wanna stay alive.' Zane jerked his jaw and gave them a menacing look. 'If there's a lawman in Jackson he'll be on the lookout for a gang of eight men riding in from Idaho. So we gotta split up. Ain't that obvious? Or do y'all fancy ropes round your necks?'

'Pah! What you so scared of, Señor Hollister? Me an' my boys, we ride in with you. We ain' scared of a few lousy gringos.'

'You!' Zane spat out in disgust. 'You durn fools. You're the ones they'll be particularly on the lookout for. Three durn Mexicans who shot up that township. There was no need for that.'

'An' what about you robbin' that bank?' Raoul returned with a sneer. 'You geev us a lousy hundred dollar each. A beeg lot more you got, that for sure. You an' your two *compadres* off to have good time in Jackson, leave us to keeck our heels.'

'Look,' Zane said, 'I'm gonna level with you.' He patted the bulging sack he had hanging from his saddle horn. 'Maybe there is another thousand or so in here. But I'm going to invest this for you. For us all. Ain't we stuck together for five years? Ain't I made the decisions, seen us through? You gotta trust me, boys. You know what I'm plannin' to do? Set up our own saloon, our own gals, whiskey galore. And be sure I got other li'l schemes in mind.

We're gonna be big shots in this valley of Jackson.'

He jerked his mustang to him and swung into the saddle. His savage countenance split into a grin. 'We'll be back to see you in a coupla days. You can trust me to come up trumps, boys.'

'Yeah.' Kenny had been perfecting his throwing skills, thudding his blade into a lone pine. He retrieved it, wiped the razor-sharp blade clean and gave the men his creepy smile. 'If you don't like it you know what you can do.'

He leaped on his horse and went chasing away down the canyon after Zane and Billy Bob. The other men stood and watched them go.

'Look at him,' Zoot moaned. 'Him and his stoopid roulette wheel.' Zane had tied the wheel to the spare horse again, which was jogging along in his wake. 'Set up a saloon? He ain't got a chance.'

'Aw, I dunno,' Jake loyally replied. 'Zane's allus been good to us.'

'You think so?' Zoot replied. 'The

whiskey sure has addled your brains, pal.'

'He should have shared that thousand dollar weeth us,' Raoul put in. 'Eef I had sense I would cut his throat last night as he slept an' taken eet for us.'

His two sidekicks, inaptly or, perhaps, hopefully christened Angel and Jesus, squatted on their boot heels by the fire and grinned agreement.

'*Bueno*,' one cried, stroking his thumb across his throat. '*Buenos noces*, Zane.'

'You wouldn't have a chance,' Jake muttered as he filled a tin mug with coffee from their battered pot. 'Zane and Billy Bob are fast. And that Kenny's even faster with his knives. We just got to hang on here, boys.'

5

Glen and Katrina had gone about thirty miles along the winding trail that followed the serpentine Snake River south.

'We'll rest the horses for an hour,' Glen said, pulling them into the side of the trail. 'And take a bite to eat.'

'Well, it'll be a relief to get off this bumpy dang thing,' Katrina cried, 'and stretch my legs.'

Glen strolled down to watch the river. It was strange to think that it would eventually race on its way for another thousand miles westwards until it joined the mighty Columbia.

When he got back Katrina was tucking into one of the cold roast goose legs he had brought, tearing it apart with her teeth. She had an amazing appetite considering she never did anything much.

'Where are all them damn animals coming from?' she asked between mouthfuls. 'What *are* they?'

'Elk. They're heading back up to the Yellowstone for the summer. They've been wintering down on the sage plains, those parts that ain't been fenced off by the ranchers. They see them as a menace.'

'So why don't you fence your grass off?'

'I guess I'll have to. Though with regret because a lot of the critters starve to death in the winter,' he replied. 'They were here before us. They've always followed this migration route.'

'But why don't we shoot 'em? There must be a thousand of 'em.'

'We do, but the few settlers round here can't eat 'em all. They're the only critters that have increased their numbers. That's probably because their natural predators, the wolves, are all but gone. The ranchers have shot and poisoned wolves to protect their herds.'

Glen tucked into his own goose leg

and pondered on the strangeness of it all.

'Personally, I'm sorry to see the wolf packs destroyed. It's a fallacy that they attack humans. There's no recorded instance of a human being killed. And they only take a few calves to feed themselves.'

'What if they took your calves; wouldn't you shoot 'em?'

'Well, they ain't here, so I don't know. But I love seeing the wild creatures. It seems a shame they should have to go.'

'You,' she laughed. 'You're just a big booby. I never heard such nonsense in all my life. What good are they to anybody? Wild creatures, indeed! What about them fearsome-looking bears we passed on the trail?'

'Brown bears? They won't hurt you. As long as you don't hurt them. And don't feed them. That's the worst thing to do. That's when they become a nuisance.'

'Hmm?' Katrina wiped her mouth

with the back of her hand and tossed her bones into the grass. 'You . . . you really are weird, aren't you. If it was up to me I'd shoot the damn lot. Come on, let's hit the trail. I cain't wait to get to Jackson and see the girls.'

* * *

Saloon-keeper Spud Murphy had a face like a baked potato, with a hefty chin, little eyeholes and a lumpy nose. In his satin-back waistcoat, celluloid collar and long apron, he stood at the window of the Crazy Bull as the shades of night fell.

'Well, look to be sure who's here,' he said as Glen Stone hauled in his wagon outside the front door.

'Who's he?' Zane Hollister asked. He had just rented his roulette table to Spud on a monthly basis on the proviso that he could claim it back when he opened his own establishment.

'We call him the Earl on account of how he's allus duded up when he comes into town. Look at him in his best suit and white shirt. It's a wonder he ain't in bow tie and tails.'

'What about that dainty bit of muslin by his side?' Zane gave a whistle of appreciation of Katrina's curves as she was helped down from the wagon by Glen, who tossed a silver dollar to the ostler to take the rig round the back to the stables. 'Whoo, she don't mind showing a bit of leg, do she?'

'She used to be my best gaudy-gal. I'm sorry I let her go but we all got fool crazy one night 'bout a month ago. The Earl there got as drunk as a lord when I spiked his beer with my best home-brew whiskey — got a still out in the woods. That moonshine's got a kick like a mule. The Earl didn't know what had hit him. You see that red-nosed old booze-hoister over there? He's the town judge. When the Earl woke up the next day he found himself wed to Katrina.'

'Yeah?'

'True. We went a bit far but he never did fit in with the boys. He ain't one of us. Know what I mean? Why, he sat in here one day *reading a book*. 'The Science of Cattle Husbandry', would you believe? That's what he learned his cow punching from. That and from poor old Hank, who sold him his ranch up at Jackson Hole.'

Katrina had come flouncing in, causing a stir among the girls, who flocked around her like chattering pigeons.

'I'm frozen stiff from sittin' all day on that damn wagon. Gimme a shot of your best whiskey, Spud. None of your cheap muck. You can keep that for the mugs.'

'Why, Katrina, 'tis good to be seein' you again,' Murphy roared, and he bustled behind the bar. 'And you, Mr Stone, sir. How's married life treating you?'

'Fine.' Glen forced a grin and waved away the bottle. 'I've forsworn all noxious liquors since a night you possibly remember. Just a root beer.'

'Aw, come on. Let your hair down,'

Katrina cried. 'We never get a chance to celebrate up at that godforsaken ranch of yourn.'

Glen shook his head and lowered his voice. 'Don't you think you ought to take it easy? We ain't had no dinner yet. And from the sound of things they're already sitting.'

There was indeed a clatter of cutlery and a chomping of teeth coming from the dining room.

'You hang on, you old stick-in-the-mud. I got some catching up to do with the gals.'

Glen was in the dark, pinstripe suit in which he had stepped off the train at Cheyenne. He only wore it when he came into Jackson. He had washed and ironed his white shirt himself, his wife considering herself a bit above such chores.

His bootlace tie had a curved longhorn toggle. He removed his wide-brimmed hat and told Murphy, 'We need a room for the night.'

'Sure.' The saloon-keeper beamed at

him. 'You can have the best in the house. I bet you'll recognize it from your last visit, eh?'

'Yes, I guess I will,' Glen replied, non-committally. 'How much do I owe you?'

'I'll put the drinks on the bill. Pay in the marnin'.'

'I'd rather pay the bar tab as we — or she — go along.'

'OK, let's see. Dat's five dollars.'

Glen gulped and reached in his pocket for his wallet. The best whiskey was going down Katrina's throat at an alarming rate.

'Looks like it's gonna be another expensive night.'

'Yes, and a bumpy one, too.' Spud beamed as he snatched the cash. 'She's buying her old pals a drink. I won't let her do dat again. They got work to do.'

Eventually Katrina whirled on him. 'Right! Let's go get dolled up and eat.'

Zane had been joined by Kenny Hayward, who had donned a worn overcoat over his ragged vest.

'Who's them two?' Kenny asked.

'Some tenderfoot from the east. We gonna have fun with that sap tonight. His lady has sure taken my fancy.'

* ★ ★ ★

The hotel, with its saloon, dining hall and bedrooms above, had been a solid, well-built edifice. But, as Murphy prospered, a warren of gimcrack rooms of three storeys had been tacked on to one side. As he grew richer he had added to the far side a dance hall and a gambling parlour, next to the saloon. Above these were the poky rooms to which the gaudy-girls, as they called them hereabouts, lured their marks like spiders lured their flies.

The fashionable sorts in the centre block must have wondered where all those screams, shrill shouts and laughter emanated from throughout the night.

Some such respectable types looked slightly startled as Katrina whirled into the best dining room, where white tablecloths sparkled with silver cutlery and tureens.

'Wow!' she yelled. 'It's a long time since I dined in style. What we gonna have? First things first.' She waved a beringed finger to a waiter. 'Hey, bring us a bottle of California red, best in the house.'

'Ain't you had enough already?' Glen hissed.

'Enough?' She laughed. 'I don't know the meaning of that word. The night is young, husband dear. I'm just gittin' started.'

Respectable ladies, both rich and poor, wed or unwed, appeared to have adopted the English Queen Victoria's taste for mournful attire; even the most fashionable were swathed in voluminous, bell-shaped dresses from neck to toe, and always wore bonnets on their heads.

So those in the dining room gave angry glances at Katrina's vulgar face-paint, her clanking jewellery and scandalous dress of turquoise taffeta revealing not only her silk-stockinged calves but most of her bosom, too. Her piquant language didn't help either.

'You know, if you're serious about being wed and a member of normal society,' Glen remarked, noticing the dagger looks, 'it might win us a few friends if you didn't go around half-undressed like some fallen woman.'

'Huh!' she jeered. 'Honey, I *am* a fallen woman and proud of it. What the hell you want me to look like? You know what they say: 'If you got it, flaunt it.' You think I'm worried about these snobs?'

'Please yourself.' He shrugged, grinning at her defiant air. 'Just an idea, thassall. I see what you mean. You look fine to me.'

'Good.' She refilled her glass with wine and raised it to him. 'I feel mighty fine, too. Here's to us.'

Murphy certainly didn't skimp on the grub. His menu ran from trout, salmon or soup to a choice of roasts: beef, venison, elk or buffalo loin, with mashed or sweet potatoes, celery and squash.

There was cranberry or apple pie and cream for dessert and Glen marvelled at how Katrina managed to pack away so much in her hourglass frame. Mind you, she did say no to coffee, jellycakes and doughnuts, finishing the bottle of wine instead.

Glen permitted himself one glass, pushed his chair back, stuck out his legs and lit a cigar. 'That was a rare treat,' he said. 'Ain't it nice to have a decent meal without having to do the cooking and washing-up as well?'

'It sure is,' she agreed, his slight sarcasm lost on her. 'What shall we do now? Take a whirl on the dance floor?'

'Oh, I dunno. Maybe we should hit the hay early? I'd liked to get reacquainted with the big comfortable bed.'

'You guys!' Her eyes sparkled with mischief as she spoke for all to hear.

'You got one-track minds. All after one thing.'

Glen blushed to the roots of his hair as she took his hand. 'Come on, Casanova. Let's go see what's going on.'

The saloon bar was packed with men: storekeepers, cowpunchers, drifters, gamblers and others of indeterminate occupation, in all kinds of costume, both snazzy and shoddy. There was even a couple of trappers in coonskin caps and buckskins who were sprawled out in front of the log fire, smoking their pipes.

Smoke? It lay in a pall, wreathing them all; fumes from noxious kerosene lamps and even more noxious tobacco mingled with the ripe aroma of unwashed males. No respectable lady would venture in here at this time of night.

'Make way, gents,' Katrina yelled, shoving through the mob. 'Got a thirst just as big as yourn.' They stood back to gawp at her as Glen eased his way behind her to the bar. 'Hey, Charlie! Two glasses of your best bourbon.' She indicated with thumb and forefinger that they should be large ones.

'Hang on a minute,' Glen protested. 'Not for me.'

'Come on.' She smiled radiantly, clinking her glass to his. 'Just one won't do you no harm. Keep you young.'

'I ain't so sure about that,' he muttered. 'Is that a polka they're playing? Come on, let's dance.'

It wasn't much of a band, just a fiddle, guitar and squeezebox, but it had a good old rumpy-ta-tumpy beat and soon he was twirling her around, among the throng, in his arms.

'You know,' she said, her lips brushing his cheek, 'I oughta charge you for this. I used to get ten cents a dance. Jeez, how my damn feet useta hurt after a night with these clod hopping varmints! To tell you the truth, you don't dance too bad.'

'You, too,' he said, and for some moments he experienced an elation, a happiness with her, a sense of everything being OK with the world. Or perhaps it was the couple of drinks he had had. 'Can I pay you another ten cents?'

They entwined fingers and waited until the music started again. He put an arm around her slim waist and spun her away. He laughed as they came to the end. 'Whoo,' he said. 'I gotta go take a leak.'

'Right.' She smiled. 'I'll still be here.'

He pushed his way out of the throng, back through the dining room, but there was no sign of any water closets, so he went out the back door. Some characters were urinating against a wall so he joined them.

'What a woman,' he muttered.

It took him a while to find his way back, but as he went to enter the saloon bar some men sort of glanced at him and moved their shoulders across, trying to block his entry to the room. Something seemed to be going on. Glen was a man of average height, about five ten, so couldn't get a clear view of what was happening. He more or less had to shoulder the men out of the way to get to the bar. Then what he saw stopped him in his tracks.

Katrina was in an amorous embrace with Zane Hollister. Not that Glen knew his name. All he knew was that a tall, hook-nosed guy in a red shirt had his arms around her and that his lips were churning on hers as the onlookers urged them on.

'Go on,' one groaned, 'give it to her.'

Zane's hand was groping her half-bare breast when he turned and caught sight of Glen Stone, but he just grinned, lecherously, and went back to kissing Katrina.

Glen's mouth had gone exceedingly dry. They were all watching him, waiting to see what this greenhorn would do.

'Take your hands off that woman,' he blurted out. 'She's with me.'

The town council, of which Murphy was the mayor, had decreed that all firearms should be handed in by men entering barrooms. Glen and, apparently, Zane had abided by the rule. So there was no question of a shoot-out.

'Waal, northern boy,' Zane drawled, 'she ain't now, is she?' He licked a lascivious tongue up Katrina's cheek as he hung on to her. 'She's from good ol' Georgia and us southerners like to stick together. See what I mean? Why don't you git lost, boy?'

The whiskey fired up within him as Glen caught hold of Katrina's shoulder, pulling her apart from the muscularly built six-footer. She did not speak, just looked at Glen with a dazed expression.

Glen's right fist shot out, aimed at Hollister's chin. But Zane was wiry and ducked aside. The young rancher caught him with his left, thudding it hard to his nose to send him falling spread eagled across a table.

He stared at Glen in surprise, wiping away a trickle of blood.

'So that's the way you want it?' He drew himself up and charged like a maddened bull. Glen sidestepped and slammed his head into the bar.

Dazed, Zane groped to haul himself upright, grabbed a bottle, smashed it and thrust the jagged weapon at Glen's face. More sober than most of the customers there, the 'greenhorn' was faster on his feet, too. He caught Hollister's wrist and twisted it to smash down on broken glass, making him yelp with pain.

Zane looked alarmed when the rancher caught him by his bandanna and gritted out:

'You want to play dirty?' Not waiting for a reply, Glen kneed him in the groin, then hurled him back at the table, which cracked under him, leaving him to sprawl amid its remnants on the floor.

Men were hollering at Hollister to get back into the affray. They had started casting bets on the outcome. There were going to be a lot of losers. Kenny and Billy Bob were kneeling beside him, urging him to retaliate.

'You can take him,' Kenny hissed, trying to secretly pass him his knife. 'Go on, cut him, Zane. Look what he's done to you. You gonna let a Yankee git away with that?'

'He won't get away.' Hollister spat out blood as they hauled him up. 'There'll be another day.'

He jerked his jaw and forced a grin. 'Whew! This boy packs quite a punch.' He offered a hand to Glen and lied, 'I guess I owe you an apology, mister. I surely had no idea this girlie was your wife.'

Glen ignored the hand and turned to Katrina, 'Come on, you've caused enough trouble for tonight.'

As he caught her arm and propelled her away through the crush of men he heard Zane call out, 'How was I to know you'd wed the saloon whore?'

Glen turned and pointed a finger at him. 'You say anything like that, or touch her again, I'll kill you.'

Out in the foyer Katrina was so unsteady he had to pick her up and carry her up the stairs. He kicked open their room door and hurled her on to the bed.

'Oh,' she squealed. 'I love it when you're mad, bad, and dangerous.'

He stared at her, shook his head sadly, and kicked shut the door.

★　★　★

When he woke at first light he put an arm across the mattress, but the space was empty and cold. 'Where'n hell's she gotten to?' he murmured to himself.

After a few minutes the door opened and Katrina, in her dressing-gown, her hair over her eyes, her lip rouge-smudged, lurched in. She had something in her arms, which she carefully packed into her bag.

'Where've you been?'

'Down to the privy. Why?'

'You've been drinking. I can smell it on you.'

She dropped her gown and squeezed into bed beside him.

'Well,' she said, smirking, 'Murphy might shutter his front doors but he don't lock the bar. So, I've been sittin' there all on my own havin' a couple of stiffeners. The hair of the dog.'

'Oh?'

'Come on, sweetheart. You're not still mad, are you? What got into you last night? It was only a little kiss. Can I help it if men fancy me?' She put out an arm to stroke his neck, but somehow he was not in the mood. 'Maybe it's you who needs a stiffener,' she said.

6

News of events at Idaho Falls had taken some time to trickle through to Jackson, maybe due to Zane's gang cutting any telegraph wires they passed on the 150-mile ride. But today the *Jackson Times* front page splurged:

Massacre . . . a dozen men killed in shoot-out . . . bank manager and woman knifed to death . . . gang escape with $6,800. Believed to be Comancheros and heading this way.

The four-page rag was selling like hot cakes. Any mention of the infamous Mexican gangs who, not long before, had roamed up from the border, killing, robbing and kidnapping white women for their brothels, filled folks with rage.

Early the next morning Kenny

Hayward was seated on the hotel's sidewalk steps whittling a bit of wood while Billy Bob read out the grisly story.

'Howdy, boys.' A big, well-padded old-timer with white hair came to stand over them. 'You two and your pal rode in here yesterday. Where you from?'

'Who the hell are you?' Kenny drawled.

The big man stroked his white moustache, spat a gobful of tobacco juice to stain Billy Bob's boot, and drew back his suit jacket to show them his badge.

'Matthew Alison, sheriff of Jackson. You ain't answered my question. We can do this the easy way or the hard way, whichever you like.'

Zane had briefed his men on what to say. They had been out on the eastern plains at Lander, delivering a herd. When they left Death Canyon they had circled around to make it look as if they had come through the pass from the prairies.

'Well, sir,' Billy Bob explained, 'that's where we been. Lander, selling a herd we druv up from Texas.'

The sheriff had watched them ride in as if from the north and was reasonably satisfied.

'Whose herd?' he asked.

'Why, Zane's. He's the boss. You better ask him,' Billy Bob whined in his southern drawl. 'You read about these Comancheros coming this way? This town don't sound safe to us. We'll prob'ly be movin' on.'

'You see any sign of Mexicans around?'

'It's funny you ask that.' Kenny put away his knife and sprang to his feet, looking the sheriff in the eye. 'We did see three yesterday when we rode in. It was back up the valley. They were on t'other side of the river, headin' across to that big gash of a canyon in the mountain wall.'

'Death Canyon?'

'Yes, sir. I do believe that's what it's called.'

'You sure about that?'

'Sure I'm sure. You cain't mistake them tall sombreros those guys wear.'

The sheriff chawed more baccy and spat again but in another direction. 'Guess I'd better raise a posse and go take a look. You boys want to come along?'

'Oh, no, suh,' Kenny said. 'We ain't fightin' men.'

★ ★ ★

Glen had got up early, harnessed the pair of horses and driven the wagon along past Jackson's cattle pens to the post office.

'About time you turned up,' the postmaster complained. 'I can hardly get in my storeroom with that durn bed there.'

It was certainly a big one with a steel sprung base and brass bedknobs.

'I'll give you a hand to get it on the wagon,' the postie added.

His wife, a skinny woman with a

97

beaky nose, had come out to watch. Glen stood back and scratched the back of his head.

'What bothers me is whether I can get it in.'

'Oh, you poor man.' She touched his arm solicitously. 'Do you mean you haven't yet? Perhaps you should see a medical man.'

Glen studied her for some moments, then shook his head. 'I'm talking about the size of the room,' he said.

The stores were opening and Glen stocked up on some necessities: a tub of axle grease, six-inch nails, a new saddle — the old one being past repair, some boxes of sulphur matches, a shovel, a barrel of flour, pots and pans, coffee beans, salt, bandages, blankets, castor oil, string, needles, thread, a packet of chewing baccy for Hank, a couple of sturdy work shirts and a set of woollen underwear for the winter, and, by special request of Katrina, a hurricane lantern with a can of kerosene. He stacked it all on the bed and drove back to the hotel yard.

Glen gave the horses their nosebags of oats to munch and called, 'Good mornin',' to a bald-headed fellow seated on a barrel outside the back door.

When he didn't reply Glen asked, 'What's ailing you, pal?'

The man's walrus moustache intensified the melancholy in his expression.

'Huh! You wouldn't be feelin' so hot if you'd just been fired.'

'Fired? What from?'

'I'm the deputy assistant cook here. Well, I was. Hey, you're the one who caused that ruckus last night. I had to clean up the broken table and glasses after you. Murphy's just accused me of stealin' two bottles of his best whiskey from the bar. It's a damnable lie. He kicked me out. Said I'd burned the bacon, too. He gits hellish mad. So I dunno what I'm gonna do.'

'Hey.' Glen had an idea. 'I'm needin' a cook and bottle-washer to work at my ranch. There's only five to cater for, so I'd expect you to help fetch water, feed the chucks, clean out the stables, maybe hang out a bit of washing.'

'Sounds like wimmin's work.'

'Yes, well my wife's of a delicate constitution and she ain't up to it.'

'Ain't really my line. Guess I could as long as you ain't 'spectin' me to break hosses or chase cows, stuff like that.'

'Aw, no. Maybe help mend a few fences. You'd be paid the same as the rest, thirty a month, all found.'

'OK, mister, you got yourself a cook.'

'Good.' Glen shook on the deal. 'Meet me here, in, say, an hour an' a half. We'll be pullin' out. What's your handle?'

'Isaac Newton.'

'Oh, right. I'm Glen Stone.'

He found Katrina in the dining room, looking somewhat subdued and more soberly dressed.

'The bacon's burned,' she said.

'Yeah, I know. I've got us a cook.'

'What? What's she like?'

'He's a guy.'

'I wanted a girl.'

'Girls are too much trouble,' he muttered, getting stuck into what was left edible of breakfast. He pulled out his wallet, withdrew several dollar bills. 'I've been over to the bank and drawn a bit out. I'm allowing us a hundred each for luxuries. You got an hour to fritter it away. The only rule is, no alcohol.'

'What?' she screeched. 'I can't get what I need in an hour. I got to try on dresses, I can't just — '

'You better get started because the wagon's loaded, bed and all. The horses are going to have a heavy haul if we're to be back by nightfall.'

'This is crazy. Why can't we stay another day? I need more than a hundred dollars. Where's the rest, you damn miser?'

'The wagon's leaving at ten thirty a.m. sharp,' Glen said, getting to his feet. 'If you ain't there, well, you're on your own.'

He remembered that he needed a spare wagon wheel and a couple of horseshoes.

'Maybe I *will* treat myself,' he said, as he looked in the window of a gun shop. 'This old Colt's as useless as a rusty gate.'

He stepped inside. 'Can I take a look at that ivory-handled Peacemaker?'

'That's their latest model, sir, only came out in '78. Designed to use .44s, the same as a rifle, so a man doesn't need to carry two types of ammunition.'

'Very nice.' Glen examined the revolver, twirled it, stuck it in his holster. 'Feels good. How much?'

'One hundred dollars, sir. Very much in demand.'

'I'll give you ninety.'

'Done.'

★　★　★

'What?' Zane Hollister demanded. 'You told the sheriff where to find them? Have you gone outa your head? How could you? Those are loyal comrades of ourn.'

'Aw.' Kenny shrugged. 'You said

yourself those three Mexicans are becoming a liability. They could lead the lawmen to us. Jake's OK but his brain's addled with whiskey. And Zoot, well, he ain't that hot.'

'You nincompoop! What if they surrender? What if they talk? That sheriff looks the sort who don't take no for an answer. Won't *that* lead 'em to us?'

'Jake and the Mex ain't the sort to surrender.'

'Let's hope so.'

'Yeah, well, you better mind what you call me, Mr Hollister, or you and me could have a fallin'-out.' Kenny's watery blue eyes glared at Zane. 'I could beat you to a pulp any day. Like that fella last night coulda done.'

'OK, Kenny, don't lose your rag. Maybe it'wasn't such a bad idea. We'll see.'

'Yeah,' Billy Bob whined. 'An' just maybe we better git ready to run.'

★ ★ ★

'I can carry my own bags,' Katrina said haughtily, hugging one to herself as they went outside. 'You go settle up with Murphy.'

'I already have.' Glen was sure he detected a clink of bottles as she swung her bag on board and patted it down. But he decided this was not the time to argue.

He climbed on to the wagon and took the reins, while Isaac helped Katrina up, then sat himself on the far side.

They went trotting out into Jackson's main street, the big horses fresh and eager, the harness jingling. But there was a lot of traffic that morning and they were slowed to a walk.

'Oh, no!' Glen's heart seemed to stop still. He had espied Susan Cousins sitting in a neatly painted four-wheel surrey beside a young gentleman in a bowler hat and four-button suit who flicked a whip at a high-stepping milk-white mare in the shafts.

'What's the matter?' Katrina followed

his gaze. 'You look like you've seen a ghost. Hey, she ain't that li'l gal you been stuck on, is she? Yes, by George, she is!'

Glen swallowed hard as Susan drew nearer. She looked more beautiful than ever, but like a different person, clad in an elegant, long-skirted costume, lilac in colour, a wide-brimmed and befeathered matching hat perched on her golden curls.

A peal of laughter came from Katrina's painted lips as they drew near.

'Ha! You really chose some stuck-up li'l bitch, dincha? Who does she think she is?'

Susan had obviously seen and heard them but her expression did not change as they passed close by. She gave not the slightest sign of recognition or of warmth, even though Glen falteringly raised a finger to his hat. Her gentleman companion glanced their way, but they might have been passing strangers for all anybody would have known.

'So that was the virgin sweetheart you were hoping would be your bride?' Katrina crowed.

'Well, she sho' is a good-looker,' Isaac opined. 'You coulda done worse.'

'Yes,' Glen gritted out. 'I suppose I could.'

It was a long, silent journey after that. Glen gave the horses plenty of rest stops. The trail was dry and firm and the pair took the strain of the heavy load well. He had travelled along it when progress was almost impossible because of snow and mud.

Katrina occasionally tried to rekindle the subject.

'The gent with her, wasn't he that shifty, double-dealing lawyer, Randolph Levick? When he first came to Jackson all he had was a soapbox to write on and a few law books. He worked at selling town lots at high prices to folks. He's done well for himself, ain't he?'

Glen still felt stunned by the sudden appearance of the couple. Levick was obviously courting Susan and she didn't seem to be averse to his charm. He refused to be drawn.

'I know nothing of him. Only met him once when I bought my land. He seemed very competent and professional to me.'

'Yeah, you can bet he is. That crafty li'l filly's landed herself quite a fish. Wonder what he's like in the sack?'

When he didn't comment she went on: 'He's a bit too slick and smarmy for me. I like 'em rough an' ready.'

'Yeah,' he muttered, 'I've noticed.'

* * *

It was twilight, the evening star glowing like a lantern in the sky, when they forded the Snake River, without mishap this time, and rattled towards the log cabins. When Glen drew in beside the stable, and Isaac jumped down, Katrina suddenly gave a spine-chilling scream and rose to her feet. 'Look!'

'Where?' Glen reached for his new revolver, jerking it out when he saw the open jaw and flashing fangs of a big grizzly bear climbing over the corral fence.

'Christ!' Isaac was scrambling for safety.

'It's all right.' The bear was unmoving; was, in fact, dead. 'It's the pelt.'

'Sorry, folks.' There was a burst of laughter behind them as Abe came out of their cabin. 'Did I give you a scare? Hank said you should be back soon so I hung on.'

Glen gave him a look. 'Must admit for moments that brute scared the pants off me again. And my dear wife.'

Abe greeted her politely, for it was the first time they'd met, but she barely gave him a glance, pushing past to go inside.

'Susan asked me to return the pelt to you, Glen,' Abe said. 'She doesn't want it in the house.'

'I saw her in Jackson.'

'Yes, she's gone to stay with her aunt for a few weeks. She seems to have take a shine to that lawyer feller.'

'Yeah, so I saw,' Glen muttered. He unharnessed the pair and found their feeding bags.

'I don't want to speak aginst your new wife, Glen, but I got to say I'm disappointed. I had high hopes our two spreads could be united under one family. They ain't big enough to be much good on their own.'

'Yeah, I had hopes in that direction, too, Abe. But it seems like it ain't to be. I'll just say I'm sorry to have let down Susan and to have disappointed you, too. Is she very bitter about it?'

'I'm afraid she is. You hurt that girl purty deep.'

'I guess so,' Glen sighed. 'You staying for supper, Abe?'

'No, I think I'll be getting home.'

'So long, Abe. You ever need any help, let me know.'

'So long, Glen. Take care of yourself.'

The young rancher watched him go, then went into the cabin.

'You call this a rabbit stew?' Isaac Newton was saying as he stirred the pot on the stove. 'It needs a few herbs and carrots.'

'It smells pretty good to me,' Glen shouted. 'Get it dished out, chef. I'll call the others in. We'll unload the wagon afterwards.'

7

The first thing Zoot Evans heard was the thudding of the ground as he tended their fire. It was getting dark and when he looked up he saw them coming, dark figures, rifles in their hands, seeming to him like the Horsemen of the Apocalypse, pounding through Death Canyon towards them.

'Jake!' he croaked, sensing disaster fast approaching. 'Watch out!'

'What?' The older man was leaning on his saddle by the fire and his first instinct was to go for his gun and roll for cover behind a boulder, leaving Zoot standing there silhouetted by the fire.

The horsemen — more than four: about twelve, in fact — came on at a headlong pace, but suddenly reined in. Their leader held up his hand, whirled his horse around, steadied himself in the stirrups and shouted,

'Hey, boy, raise ya hands. Grab air if ya know what's good for you.'

Zoot stared into the barrels of the rifles trained upon him and did as he was bid.

'Where's the rest of you?' Sheriff Matt Alison bellowed. 'Them three greasers. We know — '

He ducked in alarm as a gunshot racketed out, sending his hat flying and causing his mount to skitter away for cover.

Gunpowder flared from behind a rock as Jake wildly fired his six-gun. Just as wildly the possemen let loose a volley of lead in his direction. One of the posse got unlucky as a bullet sent him spinning from the saddle.

Zoot's last thought was that he could have talked his way out of this, but now there was nothing for it but to join in the battle. He pulled out his sidearm and raised it to fire. Before he could squeeze the trigger lead tore into his chest and sent him back-pedalling into the fire.

'Charge!' the sheriff urged his men, but made sure they all went before him. Screaming for vengeance the possemen spurred their mustangs forward as old Jake got to his feet aiming his last bullet. He had no chance. They shot him to pieces.

'Take cover!' the sheriff roared. 'Them Mexicans must be hiding . . . someplace.' He looked and listened but there was only silence and the acrid scent of curling gunsmoke. The posse rode up and down the canyon to no avail.

'They gawn,' one said, and spat into the dust. 'Or maybe they weren't here at all.'

'Hell, we shoulda kept that first fella for questioning,' the sheriff muttered. 'I shoulda told him to lie flat on his belly.'

'He drew his gun, so we had to put him down,' another posseman pointed out. 'You told us to charge. In my book that means start shooting.'

'Poor old Baker Jim.' The sheriff gazed at his body. 'To see a good man like that lose his life in the line of duty is enough to git anybody mad. We won't be eating any of his scones no more.'

'Hey,' another posseman called out, pointing to tracks on the ground. 'Looks like there definitely were more than two men here. More like eight of them.'

The others looked uneasily at each other. That meant that those Comancheros could still be prowling around out there up along in the mountains.

* * *

'Why don't you put a padlock on the cabin door?' Katrina asked. 'I don't like the idea of leaving it open for anybody to come calling. That ol' fellow the other night had certainly made hisself comfortable. I bet he had a good sniff around in my drawers.'

'Abe's not like that,' Glen replied, laughing. 'He was just being neighbourly. He had the fire going nicely for us, didn't he? That's the way we do

114

things around here. Watch out for each other.'

'I still don't like it, 'specially if I'm here on my own. A damn grizzly could come nosing in. I can't say I like everybody crowding in here to eat with us, either. There ain't room. You should tell 'em to stay in their bunkhouse.'

'It's the American way, Katrina. It's democratic. Anyhow, I enjoy their company.'

'You're the boss and you should tell them we like to eat alone. You're the one who talks about respect, but you ain't gonna get none if you let that smelly crew treat you like you're one of the gang. You gotta be more aloof.'

'For the Lord's sake, Katrina!' Glen cried with exasperation. 'The oven's in here. This is where we do the cooking.'

'Put it in the bunkhouse. Isaac can bring our meals over to us. All we need is a tin stove to keep warm and for a pot of coffee or a bit of toast.'

Glen had had a busy few days, what with running the ranch, putting the bed into the bedroom — a tight squeeze — and building a fourth log wall to enclose it.

'Anything else?'

'Yes.' She was sitting in a new peach-coloured nightdress that she had bought, which didn't leave much to the imagination. She was staring into her mirror, creaming her face, preparing for an early night. She had no interest in peering at books by candlelight, as he did. 'When we going into Jackson again?'

'Oh, I dunno. In a month's time, maybe.'

'Why don't you get a neat little buggy like your ladyfriend's boyfriend has? Then I could drive in by myself if you don't want to come. That lawyer man certainly knows how to treat a lady.'

'Katrina,' he protested, 'she isn't my ladyfriend any more. I wish you wouldn't — '

'What's that?' she exclaimed in alarm, hearing an insistent scraping at head height against the back wall.

Suddenly a knife poked away clay and moss and slid through a slight gap between two of the logs.

Their eyes widened with shock in the candlelight as a voice called through: 'Green-go, I come for your wife.'

Glen swallowed a stab of fear, got to his feet, and went to open the door. The moon had yet to rise from behind the wall of mountains but in the darkness he could see the shadowy shape of a horseman.

'Who is it?' he called.

'*Señor!*' A bald-headed Mexican in a purple serape kneed his stallion forward so that he could be seen more clearly in the light from the doorway.

He sang out, 'We poor passing strangers. We got nowhere to stay. You geev us supper an' a place to sleep, huh? Like a good Christian should.'

'Who's that maniac round the back?' demanded Glen. 'He nearly made us jump out of our skins. What the hell's he playing at?'

'Aw, that Hay-zoos,' Raoul called

back. 'He a leetle crazy.' He tapped his finger to his bald dome.

The Mexican was holding his big sombrero in front of him in a beseeching manner but Glen had an idea it might be covering a gun. He was glad he still had his holster on his belt. His fingers hovered over the ivory butt of his new Peacemaker and he thumbed back the hammer in readiness. Nonetheless, he felt mighty uneasy, for he heard another horse whinny. Then, as the bunkhouse door opened, casting light, he could see a third mounted Mexican some way back.

To tell the truth he was relieved to see Hank emerge, barefoot in his long combinations, but with a carbine held in his hands. The normal law of Western hospitality would be to allow any travellers caught out in the night a bite of supper for a small charge, and to let them bed down in a barn. But this wasn't a normal situation.

'You varmints had better clear right out,' Glen called out. 'The sooner the better. The vigilantes are out looking for you.'

'Ah, *señor,*' Raoul shrilled. 'Is that friendly when our horses are tired and ourselves hungry? Maybe your beauti- fool wife can cook up sometheeng nice and hot for us?'

'What the hell's going on?' Katrina called from inside the cabin. 'You're letting a draught in here.'

'Ah, there she is,' Raoul cackled. 'She can't wait for us to geev her a good — '

'You want any help, Glen?' Hank shouted.

'You stay out of this, old man,' the other Mexican threatened, turning his mustang to prance towards Hank. 'Or you might get the same as *she* did.'

Isaac, Jerry and Joe had poked their heads out of the bunkhouse, but as they didn't have weapons with them they backed away inside and slammed the door shut.

'I can handle this, Hank,' Glen called, but he didn't feel confident; he was wondering where the third

119

unwanted visitor had got to.

'Hey, greengo.' Jesus appeared from the side of the cabin, unshaven, grinning to reveal broken teeth. 'I tell you secret. I fuck your moth-er.'

'Oh, yeah?' Glen eyed him. 'Well, somebody obviously did but I doubt if it was you. You're too damn ugly.'

Raoul hooted with laughter. 'He funny man, eh?'

'He wan' theenk eet funny when we — ' Jesus's fingers were creeping towards the revolver in his sash.

Glen decided it was either Jesus or Raoul. And he decided on Jesus. It was the only way to shut his filthy mouth. The Peacemaker came out at great speed and he made no mistake: his first shot smashed the Mexican's mouth apart. Teeth, bone, flesh and blood rose in a fountain as he was blown by the .44's high-velocity bullet off the porch.

'Son of the Devil!' Raoul screamed, as his black stallion reacted to the crash and flash and kicked air, twisting and bucking. 'You demon!' his rider shouted, trying to control him.

The horse's terror was fortunate for Glen, otherwise he might have been the next casualty. Raoul had cast his sombrero aside to reveal in the half-darkness a nasty-looking snub-nosed shotgun pulled into the crook of his arm, his finger on the trigger.

He fought to get a bead on Glen, but cursed again as suddenly another shot crashed out to startle the horse.

It all happened almost simulta-neously, in a matter of seconds. Hank turned his carbine on Angel and fired at the dark figure, to take him out.

'You bastard!' he shouted. 'It was you — '

But the bullet whistled past Angel's cheek, as he charged his mustang and knocked Hank tumbling to the ground. As the horse stamped on the old man Angel jumped down and kicked his spurs across Hank's face and chest, raking him again and again as blood flowed.

'You try keel me, huh?' he grunted.

'For that you will die a slow death.'

The door of the bunkhouse creaked open and Jerry peeped out, a Colt in his hand. He quickly jumped back when Angel sent lead flying at him, splintering the door.

The explosions of the weapons made Raoul's stallion kick and buck some more. The Mexican pulled the cruel bit hard in to subdue the beast, then turned back to deal with Glen. He blasted the first barrel of the sawn-off shotgun at him.

Glen leapt for cover from the scattergun into the darkness. But as he did so he hit his fist against a hitching post.

'Ouch!' he yelled. He crawled about, seeking his revolver, which had gone flying.

'Where he go?' Raoul wheeled his horse and fingered the second hammer to fire another volley of lead.

Angel had leapt back into the saddle and now rode to help him. Behind them Hank crawled along to retrieve his carbine. With a huge effort he raised it. He fired. The slug hit Angel in the back. The Mexican flung up his hands and slowly lurched to one side, crying 'Holy Maria!'

Raoul wheeled back to see what was going on. As he did so Katrina came from the cabin, the Winchester hugged tight into her shoulder. 'Hey, asshole!'

The Mexican turned and saw her naked body silhouetted by the candlelight through the diaphanous nightgown. He gasped with surprise as her bullet hit him, gouging a hole through his heart.

'You — you beetch!' was all Raoul had time to say as he thudded to the ground.

Glen had found the Peacemaker and now emerged from a huckleberry bush to survey the scene.

'You! Where you been?' Katrina snarled. 'Do I have to do everything around here?'

Glen made sure the Mexicans were dead. 'In all fairness we got one each,' he said. 'You go back in. You'll catch cold.'

He went across to tend to Hank as the boys emerged from their lair. They helped to carry him back into the bunkhouse.

'You're gonna be OK, old-timer,' he said as they laid him on his bunk. 'I'll go get some bandages and hot water and we'll dress those wounds.'

'They're the same ones.' Hank reached out a quavering hand to him. 'The ones who burned me down. I'm sure of it. My wife didn't die of smallpox. They raped her and slit her throat. She has been avenged.'

'I guess I'm lucky they didn't do the same to us,' Glen said, and went back to the cabin.

Katrina was gulping back a tumbler of whiskey.

'I sure need this,' she said, offering him one from the bottle. 'Murphy won't miss it.'

Glen smiled, pouring a glass for himself. And another for Hank. He raised his to her.

'Thanks. You know, sometimes I like you. You're not as bad as you pretend to be.'

Her eyes smouldered as she assessed him.

'I wouldn't bet on it.'

8

Susan loved a hard fast ride in the morning and her filly, Birdie, never failed to oblige, with legs of iron pounding across the prairie and swerving around rocks.

'You're a little beauty,' she called, patting the dun's neck as they reached sight of Jackson town again. She jumped down, rearranging her long dress, which she had hoicked up so that she could ride astride. She adjusted the stirrup and climbed up to sit side-saddle in a more respectable manner.

Indeed, she could smell the town: its longhorns herded into the pens, its slaughterhouse, the piles of rubbish thrown out into the street. She could even catch the whiff of alcohol from the town's several saloons, outside which ruffians were sitting, sunning themselves, their faces shaded by wide-brimmed hats. They watched her, giving whistles and catcalls as she rode in.

The main street was teeming with people: hunters and trappers in greasy buckskins and furs, cowboys in canvas shirts, leather chaps and high-heeled boots; travellers, storekeepers, business-men, a sprinkling of casual visitors, or consumptives come to take the moun-tain 'cure', amid more dowdy sorts of individuals.

'Clear the way, folks!' a teamster was yelling, cracking his twenty-foot whip over the ears of his mules. He cursed luridly as he drove a heavily loaded freighter into town.

Randolph Levick came out of his office and greeted Susan.

'You look positively glowing,' he said, putting a hand out to help her down, as if she couldn't manage on her own. 'Where've you been?'

'Oh, I don't know. Along out across the grasslands. Just riding.'

'It worries me, Susan dear. Don't you

see how dangerous that could be?'

'Don't be silly,' she replied, as he held her in his arms and kissed her cheek. 'I hardly saw a soul. There were a couple of men with rifles over their mounts' necks, and game slung behind the saddles. But they were most polite and cheerful when I stopped for a chat.'

'Chat? You mustn't do that. There are some nefarious characters around.'

Soberly dressed, Levick was strongly built but his shoulders were hunched, as if from constant stooping over his desk. The dark curls on his forehead were already going thin. His long nose had a twisted droop and when he grinned he reminded Susan of some jackdaw on a branch. Once he had her in his arms he seemed reluctant to let her go.

'You must come in for coffee.'

She let Birdie drink from a trough, hitched her to a rail and was ushered into the lawyer's office, which was situated below his living quarters upstairs. There was coffee on the stove

128

and he poured two cups from the enamel pot. His secretary woman was hammering away at one of the new-fangled typewriters and gave Susan a brief smirk.

'I've a treat for you, precious. I'll just check these letters, then how about coming to see our new house?'

It was all a bit sudden to Susan. She had only known Randolph Levick for a few weeks when he had suddenly gone on one knee, produced a diamond engagement ring and slipped it on to her finger. Maybe he was 'catching her on the rebound' but she was still so furious with Glen Stone she found herself saying yes. Since then Randolph Levick seemed to have taken over her life: taking her out on drives, escorting her to his Pentecostal church, insisting that she become one of the faithful, and discussing details for the ceremony with the pastor.

He sat at his big desk, which was piled with documents and law books, as were the dusty shelves all round the room. He made some terse remarks in legal jargon to his secretary, then dipped a quill pen in ink to sign her work. 'That'll show him,' he remarked grimly. 'Have these served immediately.'

'Aren't you giving him time to pay?' the secretary asked.

'No, I've given him every chance there is. We foreclose on the mortgage.'

'Who's that?' Susan asked.

'It's not really any of your buiness, dear. The Evans lot. You know, that run-down grocery store. He can't or won't keep up his payments.'

'You mean you're putting him and his family out on the street?'

'Oh, they'll find somewhere else to go. That sort always do. Feckless, that's what they are. Money runs through his hands like water through a bucket full of holes. Come along, sweetheart. I'm a busy man.'

So they went trotting along in his fine rig to the edge of town, where quite a mansion had been raised. Labourers and carpenters were busy putting the final touches as Levick, brandishing the architect's drawings, loudly criticized their efforts.

Outside, an ornamental garden was being laid.

'We will be able to entertain in grand style out here,' he said, taking her hand to twirl her with a flourish as if she would be the centrepiece. 'I want everything to be just right for my bride.' He rasped the words into her ear as he hugged her to him from behind. 'Just look at that view.'

'Hmm?' To the west was a range of hills rising 4,000 feet above sea level. 'Not as grand as ours of the Tetons from our front veranda.'

'What are you saying? That you'd rather be on your father's ranch than here with me?'

'No, of course not,' Susan murmured, although for some reason she wanted to needle him. 'It's wonderful, Randolph. Very impressive.'

She, of course, knew nothing of the night's events fifty miles to the north, nor that in the small hours of darkness a cowboy from the Trois Tetons ranch, Jerry, had ridden in to awaken the sheriff. Only Ed Rawlings, the editor-reporter-compositor of the *Jackson Times*, had heard him. He was working late in his hut at his small Washington hand press, churning out the next day's four-page edition. He did not hesitate to join them when he heard the news, and all three set off on fresh horses.

But something had alarmed Susan.

'I'm worried about Dad. I've a feeling something's wrong. I think I must get back home.'

'What could be wrong? You were going to stay another week. Don't be silly, dear. Don't you dare go rushing off on your own. I insist I go with you. I've got to get back to see a client. Anyway, I've booked a table for dinner tonight. I want you there with me, darling, in all your glory.'

Back in town he gave her an unneeded hand up on to Birdie. 'I'll pick you up at six o'clock,' he called, as she went clipping away back to her aunt's.

★　★　★

'Whoo-ee!' Zane Hollister gave a whistle of appreciation as he stood at the window of Murphy's bar and watched the leave-taking. 'Who's that li'l sweetie?'

Kenny Hayward grinned, licking his lips lasciviously. 'I'd like to be *her* saddle.'

'You must excuse my friend, Mr Murphy. I myself, as you can see, am the epitome of a southern gentleman, but Kenny has a crude caveman's eye for the fairer sex.'

'Can't say I blame him.' Murphy laughed. 'She sure is a firecracker. Who's the lucky man? That shyster lawyer over there. They're engaged to be wed.'

'Well, she ain't wed yet.' Zeke was barely recognizable, his cheeks shaven, bar sideburns and moustache, and duded up in a brand-new check suit, double-breasted vest with a gold watch and chain and clean linen. He'd even given his boots a shine. Why have cash if you couldn't spend it?

'So, maybe,' he purred, 'I might just get a foot in the door. Where's she live? In town?'

'No, fifty miles north on the Yellowstone trail. Her daddy's got a spread on the west side of the Snake up by the string of lakes where them mountains rise sheer up outa the plain.'

'Yeah? I think I know the place. We rode past there once, don't you remember, Kenny?'

'Yeah,' Kenny gurgled. 'I remember.'

Murphy rocked with laughter again. 'That guy who gave you a damn good pasting, Zane. Remember him? He's got the ranch to the south of them. He had designs on her but they had a bust-up. To tell you the truth, I feel a mite guilty about that.'

'Him?' Zane scowled. 'Aw, I coulda taken him. I just didn't want to cause a scene.'

'All the more reason,' the pugfaced Kenny said, leering, 'to stick your foot, or whatever, through her door.'

'You know, just across from them, about five miles away, would be the perfect spot to open a roadhouse. At the meeting point of the trail down from Yellowstone, the one in from Lander and the east, and the one winding up from Jackson.'

'Yeah?'

'Sure.' Murphy had told Zane there was too much competition by way of saloons in Jackson. 'Yes, ideal for you. Not much good for cows, too rocky. But you could use those rocks to build the foundations and a good chimney. For timber you just fell the pines.'

'Who owns it? How do I buy the land?'

'Sure, you don't buy nuthin'. You just claim it. I can put you in touch with a gang of labourers. They'd have the place up and running within a month. And I've heard the lumberyard's got some weathered hickory. T'would make a fine bar. Gambling den, eating-house, a few rooms on top — ' Spud winked at them as he was called away. 'You could have a fine old time.'

'Hey!' Zane slapped Kenny's shoulder. 'Sounds just the place for us.'

Kenny punched air and gave a rebel yell. 'Let's drink to that, pard.'

Sheriff Matt Alison had arrived along with the editor of the *Jackson Times*. 'A fine mess ye've got here,' he observed. He took a bite of a plug of baccy, stuck the plug back in his suit pocket and stood surveying the scene. 'Maybe you'd care to explain.'

Glen did so, re-enacting the battle, pointing to the corpses who had been left all night where they fell. There was not a lot left of Jesus's head. His corpse was in the bushes and it looked like a fox had been having a go at his entrails, too.

'He was pulling his gun,' Glen said. 'I beat him to it by a hair's breadth. It was a fair draw.'

'How about this 'un?' Ants were

running back and forth over Angel, taking a peek in his mouth, which was still open in a final rictus of pain. The sheriff turned him over with his boot. 'Shot in the back.'

'Oh, yes,' the press man sang out. 'People don't like that.'

'It was lucky for me Hank got a shot in. He had been stomped on and spur-raked. He was in a bad way and still is.'

'Why lucky for you?' Ed said.

'Because they were trying to finish me to get at Katrina. You can imagine what they had in mind for her.'

'Ah, yes.' The reporter scribbled in his notebook. 'Indeed, I can.'

'Good, I'm glad you understand it was a desperate situation here. I've never killed a man before. I can assure you of that. But I — we — had to. It was them or us.'

The sheriff examined Raoul. The crows had pecked out his eyes.

'So how about him?'

'I got him.' Katrina came from the

cabin, painted and dressed as if for a dance hall, a cigarette in her lips. 'So how about the reward money, Matt, you fat slug? How much do I get? Don't think you can go claiming it for yourself. That monkey I got was obviously the main man. There must be a reward on him. A wad of it, I bet.'

'Well, howdy to you, Katrina,' the sheriff said in greeting. 'Marriage hasn't changed you much, I see. Reward? I'll have to negotiate with the bank. Seems like they was a branch of Wells Fargo. But what they're interested in is recovery of the six thousand five hundred dollars. What you got here? Six hundred dollars from the three of 'em. Peanuts. I'll have to return that to the bank.'

'What?' She daggered streaks of smoke from her nostrils. 'You chisellin' — '

'Hey!' The sheriff raised a hand, restraining a slight smile. 'No bad language to a law officer or I might have to take you in. The question is,

138

where's the rest of the loot gotten to?'

'How should we know?' she cried. 'That's your job.'

'OK, I've seen enough here. Why don't you do something useful, woman, like go boil up a pot of coffee on the stove? Or don't you sully your hands with tasks like that?'

'Go boil your head.' Katrina flicked the cigarette end at him and returned to the cabin.

Glen was about to protest at the sheriff's rudeness, but he guessed he knew her as well or better than Alison did.

'Hank's in the bunkhouse,' he said. 'I expect you want to interview him.'

'Yeah. Bring your notebook, Ed. I want you to get this down and let me have a copy for the coroner.

It was late in the day, the sun already melting behind the roseate peaks as if bloodily pierced by their tips, and as it did so deep shadow spread towards the cabins.

'You want to stay the night, Sheriff?'

Glen asked, as they came from the bunkhouse.

'Yeah, thanks. We've had a long ride. The old fellow don't look too good, does he? It'll take time but he should pull through.'

He took a last look at the corpses on the ground, now stiff with rigor mortis and the frost. He spat baccy juice on Angel's face.

'Looks like we'll have to break their damn backs to hang 'em over their hosses to take 'em into town. They're stiff as boards.'

'That's a fine stallion.' Glen looked across to where the horse was prancing around the corral. 'You usually put ownerless ones like that up for auction for town funds, don't you? I've taken a fancy to him. Could I put in a reserve bid of a hundred dollars?'

'That animal's worth two hundred bucks.' Matt Alison slapped him on the shoulder. 'I've come to the conclusion you're an honest and brave young fellow. He's yours.'

'You mean it?'

'Sure, forget the hundred tag. I'll swap him for one of your ten-dollar mustangs.'

'Thanks, Sheriff. I can smell dinner cooking. It'll be a tight squeeze but I'd be honoured if you'd join us. You, too, Mr Editor.'

'Call me Matt,' the sheriff said. 'And him Ed. There's one thang that bothers me. There's three of them desperadoes still on the loose. They might be still around. So you better stay on the alert. If I was you I'd invest in some more firepower.'

'What do you mean?'

'Hire a couple of men who can shoot. Them three in the bunkhouse seem about as much use as cat's piss on your Sunday suit.'

'Aw, none of us are fast guns but I figure we can manage.'

'Suit yourself, it's your funeral.'

9

Susan was attacking, as daintily as she could, a slice of duck breast in the Crazy Bull dining room when Randolph Levick gripped her thigh beneath the table. Susan's knee jerked in an involuntary kick.

'I wish you wouldn't do that,' she squealed.

'Why not?' He grinned at her as he brought up his hand and resumed eating. 'Don't you like me touching you?'

'It makes me jump. Oh dear, it's so hot in here I think I'll take this silly hat off.'

'No, you mustn't do that.'

'Why?' She raised her outstretched hands and gazed at the ceiling. 'It's not raining in here, is it?'

'Ladies keep their hats on when they're out. It's social etiquette.'

'But we're not out. We're in.' She fiddled with the hatpin, pulled off the feathered felt creation and tossed it on to the free chair that she had almost kicked over. She shook out her curls. 'That's better.'

'Have some more wine.' Levick had had a word with Murphy beforehand. The bottle contained a mixture of red wine and cocaine. Quite legal in those days. 'It's Vin Mariani. President Grant's favourite tipple.'

'No thanks,' she giggled. 'It's made me feel funny.'

'Go on.' He refilled her glass. He was determined tonight to break down her defences. 'Talking of presidents did you know our present incumbent, Mr Chester Arthur, is visiting the Yellowstone this summer? We could take a trip up there. I've just been elected chairman of Jackson Chamber of Commerce so there's every chance I, and you as my wife, will be introduced to him. That's certainly an honour, eh?'

'Mm.' Susan abandoned her battle

with the duck and pushed her plate away. 'I don't think I'll bother with pudding.'

Her mind began to drift as Randolph, in a loud voice to impress the other diners, recalled how he had come from a poor home, left school at twelve, swept the floors in an attorney's office, risen to be a humble clerk copying writs all day in longhand, but had studied at night school until he passed his law examinations.

She had already heard the story five times and wondered how many times she would have to listen to it in their lifetime of marriage.

Her lilac dress was tightly buttoned up to her throat. 'How fortunate I am to have a twenty-inch waist,' she murmured, interrupting his flow.

'What's that?'

'How awful it must be to be strapped into those bodices and corsets,' she exclaimed. 'And those ridiculous bustles. How can they sit down in them?'

'With difficulty I expect,' he replied, and laughed, squeezing her fingers. 'You know, we could always stay here overnight. Shall I have a word with Murphy? How about tonight?'

'What? Sleep together? But we're not wed.'

He waved his fingers to her to lower her voice and did so himself. 'Adjoining rooms,' he hissed. 'But with a communicating door. I really think we ought to get to know each other more . . . more intimately before we're married. Some brides, I've heard, get a terrible shock on their wedding night. Never get over it.'

'But wouldn't that ruin my reputation? Surely you wouldn't want that, Randolph?'

'Murphy's very discreet. Nobody would know.'

'We would. So would the staff, the chambermaids. What about my aunt?'

'Bother your aunt. Can't you see what you're doing to me? You're so adorable. I can't sleep. I want you so much. You're making me ill. Darling,' he begged, grabbing her hand again. 'Please.'

'Oh, I wouldn't bother about practising for the wedding night. I was brought up on a ranch. I've a pretty good idea of the basics.' She laughed. 'You'll just have to wait. Why? Do you make a habit of booking in here? You seem to know a lot about it.'

'No, of course I don't,' he snapped. 'It's just that you won't name the wedding day.'

'Oh, really, Randy. It's just that I'm gonna be hellish busy the next few weeks. It's the spring roundup. I've got to get back to help Dad and the boys.'

'That's not work for a young lady.'

'It's great fun. Chasing the cows out of the canyons, heading them home. I can rope and ride better'n most men. I'm not keen on the castrating, though.'

Levick winced. 'Finish your wine. Shall we go over to my office for a nightcap? Or a coffee.'

Oh, golly, she thought, as he paid the

bill. Not another hour wrestling on his office couch trying to restrain his hot hairy hands. Like the evening before. And the one before that. Yes, it seemed so, for when they emerged into the fresh air he grabbed her tightly, pulled her into the shadows and tried to plaster his lips on hers. Susan turned her face away to avoid the wet kisses.

'Not tonight, Randy. I'd better be getting back. I feel most odd. It must be that wine you gave me.'

'Damn!' he snarled, after he'd dropped her off at her aunt's and whipped the rig away. 'I've never known a gal keep her legs so tight closed. She doesn't seem to realize how lucky she is to get me. Maybe I'd better try Murphy's.'

⋆　⋆　⋆

It had been a convivial evening spent in the crowded cabin before Ed and the boys went off to bed down in the bunkhouse. Glen woke at the first glimmer of dawn and found Matt rousing himself from the cot. He tossed the blanket aside and pulled on his hat, suit and boots.

'Mornin', Sheriff. You said you want to make an early start.'

'Yeah, Ed wants to get his — or your — story out. I'll go rouse him. We need to get them stiffies and hosses ready.'

'I'll boil up some coffee, bring it out.' Glen knelt to rekindle the glowing embers in the oven as Katrina emerged from the bedroom in her long night-dress. It clung to her top half, the nipples of her breasts tightly pressed against the material.

'What's going on?' she asked, with a yawn.

'Honey,' Glen called, glancing at her. 'Couldn't you put a wrap on? Make yourself decent?'

'Aw, it'd take more'n a wrap to make me decent.' She laughed. 'Eh, Matt?'

'So long, Katrina,' the sheriff abruptly replied. He picked up his guns and went outside.

He and Ed were more or less ready

by the time Glen came out with mugs of hot coffee.

'I've packed you a bit of cold venison to keep you going,' he told the pair.

When Ed went back to the bunkhouse to find his notes Matt drawled, 'You know a lot of ranchers have married hookers. Most women settle down, make a decent life for themselves. Of course, they don't advertise their past. They don't want folks telling the gran'kids 'bout what granny got up to when she was young.'

'What you saying, Matt? That Katrina ain't like that?'

'That was a fool thang the judge did that night, marryin' you two.'

'We were all full of corn. I'm trying to make the best of it, Sheriff.' Glen looked up at the stars still glimmering in the sky and sighed. 'Aw, I know we ain't two of a kind. I love it out here in the wilds. She likes fashions, the bright lights. But in some ways we're just fine. She's a sexy lady.'

'Yeah, so I heard.'

'Oh?' Glen had feared at the time that Katrina was overdoing the sound effects for the sheriff's benefit. 'Sorry.'

'Look, pal, I don't wanna be a Jeremiah, but sex ain't everything in a marriage. And I ain't sure Katrina really enjoys it. There's some wimmin forever looking over the fence. They just cain't get no satisfaction.'

'You sayin' Katrina's like that?'

'I hope not, but what I'm sayin' is if anything should go wrong, don't get crazy mad. Don't do nuthin' stupid. I'd hate to be the one to organize your hanging.'

The late Raoul's silver engraved saddle and bridle was hanging over the corral rail. Matt Alison looked across at the spirited stallion.

'See them rowel scars on his sides? That hoss has been bad rid. I reckon he came all the way from Mexico. So he's yourn. You can have the saddle, too. It sorta suits him. So, Mr Stone, why doncha sling it on him?'

'Hey, boss, he yourn now?' Isaac

Newton had joined them. 'You gonna git on that devil?'

'Yassuh, he sho' is,' Joe whooped. 'Go on, Glen. Show him who's boss.'

Glen had planned to leave it to a later time when he could soothe the stallion, get him used to him. The creature was stamping and snorting, staring across as if defying his new captors.

'OK.' The rancher felt so fired up by the sheriff's lecture that he stepped through the rails, grabbed a lariat tossed to him and advanced. 'Come on, boy,' he coaxed.

The stallion took off round the corral, turning when he saw Glen to charge back again, his head high, mane tossing, kicking out his deadly back hoofs.

'Go on!' Katrina had put a robe on and come to watch the show. He heard her shrill jibe. 'What you scared of, Glen?'

He bit his lip, waiting his chance as the stallion reared up over him, flailing his forehoofs. The lariat went spinning over his head and dropped over his neck. Glen jerked it tight, hanging on as the horse fought to escape, the rope searing his hands.

'Right!' the young rancher shouted. He dived in and wound an arm around the muscular neck, his boots kicking dust as the devil horse tossed him about as if he were no more than a child. But his grip slipped and he went flying back, landing on the ground as the horse tried to stomp on him. He rolled clear beneath the rail and gasped, 'You're asking for it!'

He rolled back into the corral and picked himself up. The horse was angrily charging around. Glen caught the trailing lasso and, by sheer might and determination, hauled him close. Quickly he wound the rope tightly about the central stubbing post.

'Gotcha, pal.'

Glen went to get the silver-horned saddle and met Matt Alison's eyes. 'I like a hoss with a bit of spirit,' he said with a grin.

He tried to soothe the horse, stroking

his shuddering flanks, easing a blanket and then the saddle over his back. 'I ain't gonna hurt ya. Us two gonna be friends.' But the stallion didn't seem to believe him, tossing and tugging and trying to get away.

'Come on,' Glen coaxed, rubbing his mane. As the horse opened his mouth and bared his teeth, Glen slipped the spade bit in and buckled the bridle tight.

'All ya gotta do now is ride him,' the sheriff drawled.

'Open the gate,' said Glen. He loosened the lariat, tossed it aside and tightened the cinch a notch. As the stallion leapt away he swung aboard, stuck his boots into the bentwood stirrups and hung on for dear life as the horse bucked high.

'That's enough!' he cried. He kept the reins tight until the horse quietened down, realizing he wasn't going to get this man off his back just yet. 'Come on, let's go.'

The boys and even Katrina whooped

with excitement as Glen aimed at the gate and went charging away. He leapt a fence and galloped away across his range, veering through his cows, giving the stallion his head, just hanging on for the sheer joy of it.

The sheriff and his cadavers had trailed away by the time he got back after a ten-mile circuit.

'What you gonna call him?' Isaac asked. 'Satan?'

'No. 'Glen patted the stallion's neck. '*Amigo*. That's what he's gonna be.'

10

When Susan awoke she lay and thought about how light-headed she had felt the night before. Had her fiancé been trying to drug her with that drink? Randy was getting much *too* randy for her liking. It was all very well for him. He wasn't the one who might end up with a baby. What if she gave in to him and conceived? Would he still keep his word and marry her? Or was he a cad?

'Anything the matter, dear?' Aunt May asked over breakfast. 'You ain't your usual sunny self. You seein' Randolph tonight?'

'I guess so,' Susan muttered. 'He wants me to go to a church meeting.'

'That should be good.'

'Will it? I'm not sure I like that church. All that speakin' in voices. It's weird. The pastor preaches that it's good to make money, to get rich so you can be a benefactor to the poor. He's twisted the teachings of the Lord in my opinion. I guess that's why Randolph likes it. He'll come out after, rubbing his hands, making business deals. Sometimes I think that's the only reason he goes.'

'Oh, you are down in the dumps today. I mean, all that twaddle in the Bible about 'the eye of the needle'. You can't really take it literally. Your father makes money, don't he? He's a good man. Making money, being a success is the American way of life.'

'I suppose so, but Mr Levick goes on about it so. He told me he charges high prices so people will think he's the best. That seems a wee bit odd to me. And he showed me his property portfolio. He owns half this damn town.'

'Language, Susan! What you need is a good ride on Birdie. Clear your mind. Mr Levick's just the man you need. I'm sure you'll both be very happy.'

'Hmm. Maybe.'

She didn't feel much like riding and

pottered about the house most of the day, helping her aunt bottle preserves. The *Jackson Times* wasn't delivered by the boy until mid-afternoon and then her aunt came bustling in.

'Look at this. Glen's quite the hero. *And* his wife.'

'What? Let me see.'

GUNFIGHT AT THE TROIS TETONS RANCH, the headline blared. THREE COMANCHEROS KILLED.

'Goodness!' Susan glanced at the sub head: RANCHER AND WIFE FIGHT OFF DASTARDLY ATTACK. Avidly she read the report.

'I've got to get back. There's three more of the gang out there somewhere. I'm worried about Mother and Dad.'

She raced upstairs and ripped open the bodice of her new lilac dress, making buttons pop. She kicked it away, found her boy's denim jeans, tugged them on, then her boots. An embroidered shirt, her buckskin jacket and flat-crowned Stetson and she was ready.

'No, be sensible,' Aunt May protested. 'It's getting late. It will soon be dark. I forbid you, Susan. What shall I tell Randolph?'

'Tell him . . . ' The girl stood and recalled the night before when she had been in the Crazy Bull, had peered along at the raucous scene in the bar. That was where it had happened: Glen getting drunk, meeting Katrina, waking in bed upstairs with her. And Randolph Levick had pestered *her* to go up there, possibly or probably lie in the same bed as they had. She took off the engagement ring and placed it on the sideboard.

'Give him this. Tell him I want to think it over.' She sighed. 'Men! I've had enough of them. They're all the same. And I've had enough of riding side-saddle. It gives me a pain in the neck.'

She rode Birdie astride out of town, uncaring who saw her. She could have been a young cowboy heading back to his ranch. So what if it got dark? It would be a clear night. All she had to do was follow the winding white-dust trail northwards.

'Come on, girl.' She leaned forward to pat the dun's neck. 'We can do it. We're going home.'

★ ★ ★

'Hey!' Kenny Hayward was sitting on the steps of the Crazy Bull. 'You see that? That ain't no cowboy. That's that li'l filly on her filly. I'd recognize that backside any place. Now's my chance to have some fun.'

Billy Bob protested faintly. 'Ah don' thank thass a bright idea, Kenny.'

'Don' say nuthin' to Zane or nobody.' Kenny licked his lips, grinned and stuck his knife in his boot. He winked at Billy Bob and jumped on to the saddle of his mustang. He pulled it away from the hitching rail and rode at a fast lick out of Jackson.

'I wonder where she thinks she's off to?' he said to himself.

'You want to step over to the jailhouse with me for a little chat?'

Zane Hollister was in the middle of a poker game in the Crazy Bull. He looked up at the bulky sheriff.

'You got anything to say to me, why don't you spit it out here? Cain't ya see I'm busy?'

'You can either come willingly or I'll drag you across in irons.'

'Aw, hell. I was on a winning hand.' Zane tossed the cards down in disgust and got up to go with the law officer. 'What's this all about?'

'Just a few questions, Mr er . . . Green, is it?' Sheriff Alison took his comfortable swivel-chair when they reached the jailhouse and pointed to a small hardwood one in front of his desk. 'You got any proof of that?'

'What, my name? You think my ma had time to go git a birth certificate when you damn Yankees were burning our cabin down about our heads?'

'Where was that?'

'Georgia. Ain't you heard the song, Sheriff? The damn bluecoats came marching through killin', rapin', burnin', lootin', runnin' off our pigs and cows from Atlanta to the sea. One hundred million dollars worth of damage, that's what you did on that little spree.'

'And your daddy made you vow to take vengeance when you was big and rape and loot and burn down the cabins of Yankees? Ain't that so?'

'What?' Zane stopped his tirade. It was as if he had run into a brick wall. How did the sheriff know that? 'No,' he protested. 'Of course he didn't. We were a God-fearin' fambly.'

'You sold a herd in Lander? You got a bill of sale?'

'Nah. It was only five hundred head. We didn't bother.'

'Silly of you, Mr . . . er . . . Brown. Men who cain't show a bill of sale often get strung up as rustlers round here. Who you sell them to?'

'Green. That's my name, Sheriff. That feller's name. Charlie . . . er . . . somebody. I cain't remember now.'

'Maybe you oughta start to remember. This fella Charlie. How much he pay you?'

'Coupla thousand dollars.'

'You still got that?'

'Sure, most of it. Maybe you've heard I'm building a roadhouse. So I've spent a lump out on that.' Hollister grinned, trying to seem amused. 'And lost a bit on the cards. A tad more now thanks to you.'

'Where'd you buy those cows?'

'That I *do* know. The Southern Cattle Company, Miles City. Fattened 'em up fer a bit. Made a nice profit. Is that aginst the law in Jackson? Look,' he started to his feet, 'I'm gonna go git that attorney in here to represent me.'

'Siddown.' Matt Alison's expression didn't change. 'You an' your two sidekicks been through Idaho Falls lately?'

'Never heard of the place. Never

162

been west of Wyoming in my life. We done some gold prospectin' up in Montana. That's the furthest west we been.'

'You say you never heard about how an old lady and a bank manager got stabbed and several cowboys got gunned down at Idaho Falls? It was front-page news.'

'Oh, that.' Zane perched on the uncomfortable chair. 'Yeah, I did hear somethang about that. Look, where's this getting to?'

The sheriff pencilled some notes on his pad. 'So, Mr Grey, you claim to be a respectable southern gentleman?'

'Yes, I am,' Zane shouted, getting flustered. 'The name's Black — I mean Green.'

'Ah, Green. Not Brown. I must remember that. You can go.'

'What?' Zane jumped up and stomped to the door. 'Well, thanks very much, Sheriff.'

When he had gone a Wells Fargo agent, who had been listening in an adjacent cell, came in.

'You gave him a pretty easy time.'

'I don't want to frighten him off. Give him enough rope he'll hang himself.'

'Well, we don't have much to hang him with right now. All the stolen money was in used notes. No identifying serial numbers known. And he's not the only cattleman, or rustler, call him what you like, who's arrived in Jackson lately with a pocketload of cash to spend.'

'And I ain't got no mugshots on any of 'em,' the sheriff added. 'That robbery was across the line. It ain't my patch. So if you think I'm gonna waste my time writing letters to our various institutes of criminal insanity like San Quentin or Yuma penitentiary asking if a Mr Zane Green was a graduate of theirn lately you're mistaken.'

'That's all right, Sheriff. Thanks for your help. I got a hunch we're on the right trail. Sooner or later they're gonna be up to their old tricks.'

'I only hope it ain't too much later. I don't wanna find another female with her throat slit.'

* * *

Billy Bob was sitting on the steps of the Crazy Bull looking worried. 'Did he give you a rough time, Zane? What did he want?'

'Aw, just a few routine questions, Billy Bob. Guess he has to. No rough stuff. He's scared I'll set the lawyer on him. Fancy a beer? Where's Kenny?'

'Dunno. Gawn off. Dunno where. You know Kenny. He don't say much.'

'Yeah, well, I hope he's behaving himself.'

Zane led Billy Bob into the saloon of the Crazy Bull and seated him at a secluded table where they could talk. He returned with two brimming glasses of pale Pittsburgh beer.

'I'm a respectable businessman now. We got to watch our step.'

'Didn't we better get out?' Billy Bob

greedily slurped his beer. 'That sheriff. He looks mean. D'ya think he's on to us?'

'No, why should he be? Those highway robberies we pulled up in Montana, we allus wore hoods, same as when we attacked that gold wagon. They got nuthin' on us up there. We had to run due to those stupid Mexicans. The vigilantes would have hung us all. But we didn't do nuthin' to that girl. A bit of rustling before that in Wyoming. We covered our tracks. There's nuthin' to worry about, Billy Bob. You're my cousin. Ain't I looked after you so far?'

'But what if that sheriff leans on me?'

'You just stick to our story. We come up from the South four years ago. Coupla years in Wyoming cowboying. Coupla years in Montana diggin' fer gold. Sold a herd in Lander. Then we come here. We ain't never been to Idaho. You got that?'

'Coupla years Montana . . . never been to Idaho.'

Jeez, Zane thought, *this kid's our weak link. He ain't too bright.* 'Mind you,' he muttered, that sheriff did git me a tad rattled. Almost forgot what name I'd give. Green, that's me.'

'I told him I was Billy Bob Brown.'

'What?' Zane croaked. 'What about Kenny?'

'I think he said he was Snowy White.'

★   ★   ★

Kenny hung half a mile back as the girl went on at a fast canter, unaware that she was being followed. On and on she went for twenty miles or so. Since leaving Jackson they had barely seen a soul and that was the way Kenny liked it. But as he came over a rise in the trail there was no sign of her ahead.

'Funny,' he said. 'Maybe she's gone over to them cottonwoods.'

It was the only clump of greenery on the rocky heath. In the afterglow of the sunset night was falling fast. Kenny circled away from the trail until he came up to the back of the big trees. He dismounted and led the mustang beneath the spreading branches. He flicked the reins over some low-hanging twigs, which would normally be enough to restrain the horse. He had heard her voice. He slid up through some bushes and peered over some white boulders.

'Whoo!' he whispered.

There was an open glade and the girl was bent over, her back to him. She must have been talking to the pony, who was cropping grass beyond her. What had elicited the 'Whoo!' was the sight of the girl's shapely bottom pressed tight against her faded denim pants. Kenny's mouth watered as he watched, his grimy fingers wandering to his crotch as he imagined the things he was going to do. This was the best part. The start. Before it began. Drooling over her. What was she doing, bending over, holding something down in her hands? Never mind what *she's* doing. It's what *I'm* gonna be doing . . .

Suddenly Susan turned and he saw

her vivid blue eyes in the moonlight. Her bosom stretched out her blouse as she seemed to stare straight at him, then raised the Smith & Wesson .44 gripped by both her hands. Her finger on the trigger. She was only twenty paces away and Kenny seemed unable to move as he stared into the deathly hole of the barrel. The hammer hit home and with a flash and crash a bullet was expelled, chiselling the rocks a few inches from his face. Crash! Another one. And another, whanging around him, whistling away.

Kenny slid back into cover as another two shots showered him with shards of rock and almost took his scalp off.

'Christ!'

There was silence. He forced himself to peer over the rock again. She was calmly reloading, as cool as could be. Kenny reached for the knife in his boot, suddenly unsure what to do. Would she try to shoot him again? For moments he knew a shiver of fear. He was no longer the hunter. She was. His confidence was shaken. If he hurled the knife and missed . . . ?

What now? Susan stuck the revolver in the holster of her gunbelt, leapt on the pony and went jogging away out of the grove. Kenny looked around for his mustang, intent on pursuit. But the horse had bolted, tearing away from the bushes, terrified by the noise and ricocheting bullets.

'Where's the bastard gawn?' Kenny cursed. He shouted for the horse, stumbling after him, but he had disappeared into the darkness.

Susan went on at a canter, pleased with the practice session. The cotton wool stuffed in her ears had softened the blasts, masked the scream of the mustang's whinnies as he pounded away. Apart from a creepy sensation up her spine she had no idea that she was being watched. Or that she had nearly killed a man who now vowed to kill her.

'My aim's getting better,' she called to Birdie. 'It's not perfect but I hit that white rock.'

The double-handed grip suggested by the man in the gun shop who sold her the Smith & Wesson was a good idea. It helped deal with the kick of the heavy revolver. She had been shown how to handle it in the back yard of the shop, but had only got two bullets in the lifelike rag doll tied to the post.

'Aim for his belly button and you'll hit him in the head,' he had said.

'Yes, I'm definitely getting better. That was a good idea,' she called out. Well, they all said she ought to have protection out in the wilds. *I don't s'pose I'll ever have to use it for real*, she thought.

*   *   *

Kenny Hayward's lurid cusses rang through the night as he finally abandoned the search for his mustang, stumbled back to the trail and set off on foot back to Jackson. A long and blistering twenty miles away. It was almost dawn when he limped into

171

town. He was soaking his feet in a horse trough when Murphy opened up.

'What happened to you?' he asked.

'The sassy li'l Cousins bitch tried to shoot me, scared off my hoss.'

'Who could blame her?' Spud roared with laughter as he swept the steps. 'If she saw an ugly little runt like you on her tail?'

Kenny staggered past him and up the stairs to his poky room. 'She an' me'll meet again,' he muttered as he collapsed on his cot.

11

A horse preacher had arrived in town. New on the scene, he took his stand haranguing the population as they passed by, promising them they would burn in hell if they didn't change their wicked ways and 'Come to the Lord.'

Repentance Rathbone didn't have the mean, lean, grim-faced looks of many a churchman. He was tubby, rosy-cheeked, curly-haired and grey-bearded, rigged out in a colourful costume of buff-hide hat, coonskin coat, high boots and Shoshone beads. He said he travelled from ranch to far-flung ranch lassoing souls. That was probably why he looked so well fed, for he would be paid for his sermons with supper and bed.

Halfway through the morning he got off his horse and stomped into the

Crazy Bull. 'Repent, ye sinners,' he hollered. 'Know ye not how alcohol has been the ruin of too many a man?'

'What's your poison, parson?' The burly Murphy wiped the bar and grinned at the early drinkers. 'Whiskey or beer?'

'It sure gives a man a terrible thirst doing the work of the Lord,' Repentance replied. 'Make mine a beer.'

When it was served he grunted, 'I thank you, sir. Ye'll be rewarded in heaven.' He joined in the general chat along the bar, asking about beef prices and the weather and suchlike. Indeed, he seemed such a jolly chap that several stood him another drink until he announced:

'Gentlemen, do I hear the chatter of female sinners somewhere?'

'They're in the dance hall,' a storekeeper said. 'Go try your luck, Horse Preacher.'

'Aha!' Repentance cried, as he spied a half-dozen dozy girls sprawled about on chairs and a horse hair sofa. 'Fear not, ye poor fallen creatures. I'm God's messenger sent forth to bring ye back into the fold of righteousness.'

'Piss off.' The puffy-faced, exceedingly fleshy Sally Spice picked her nose and flicked what she found at him. 'Go stick your head in another dungheap, you mealy-mouthed sonuvabitch.'

'A dungheap, that's exactly what this is. I knew so. I could smell it. Fear not, ladies. I come not from any established church. I have dipped into each of them and offer you a mixture of plums. Thus, I can offer you a Roman Catholic confession to purge your souls, or baptize your heads with holy water like the Methodists do. All I ask is a small offering in my collection tin.'

This brought forth ribald ripostes from the assorted prostitutes.

'Pay you?' a skinny one screamed. 'It's you who should be payin' us.'

'Now then,' the travelling preacher soothed, patting the brow of each scantily clad female. 'I understand your woes and how you have been misused at men's hands.'

He paused in front of a girl of fifteen years or so in a cotton shift and rumpled stockings.

'What brings you here, my angel? How did you stray into this temple of sin?'

'I am an orphan, sir. My ma, pa, brother, sister, dead of the cholera. I had nowhere else to go. At least it's warm and out of the cold. I'm paid a few cents to dance with gentlemen.'

'Is that all you do, girl?' Repentance boomed. 'Come now, don't lie to a messenger of the Lord.'

'No, sir, I swear . . . well, sir, I . . . ' the girl stuttered and burst into tears.

'Alle-lu-jah!' Repentance whooped and grabbed a jug of flowers from the windowsill. 'Kneel, girl. I will wash away your sins.' He tipped the water and flowers over her head. 'In the name of the Father, the Son and the — '

'That's enough of that, ye ould fraud,' Murphy bellowed through the doorway. 'It's time these beauties were getting their glad rags on. We got a busy day ahead.'

★   ★   ★

Glen Stone rode on Crackers across meadowland beneath the high-peaked mountain range towards the Black River. He heard the sound of the falls growing louder, felt cool spray in the air. For the past weeks he had been trying to bond with the big stallion and had somewhat neglected Crackers. But Glen was seeking supper, a rifle at the ready, and a quiet ride like Crackers was just the job.

He paused at a deep pool beneath the falls, gazing down at speckled trout hanging on the current above the pebbles on the bottom. A cool green light was reflected from lichen on the boulders. On other days he would have loved to watch as he flicked a line, teasing them to take the bait. Just one of them would have made a tasty meal for himself.

But Katrina and the boys wanted meat, so he nudged Crackers on through an overhang of willows. Still in the shadow of the trees he spotted a herd of mule deer on the water's edge and drew the horse in. They were named for their twitching lop ears, like a mule's, but otherwise had nothing in common with that sturdy animal. Small, delicately formed and graceful, they would have wintered in the Hole and were heading up to seek summer grazing in the high mountains.

The hunter tugged the Winchester into his shoulder and carefully took aim along the sights at a well-formed doe. He tried for a heart shot behind the near foreleg. The well-trained horse barely started as the bullet clapped out. The herd set off, racing away, circling, leaping the rocks at great speed. The doe went with them for some yards, then stumbled and fell. When Glen reached her she was dead. He slung her behind the saddle and headed back towards the cabins. She would provide some tasty roasts for the week ahead.

★   ★   ★

In the evening he wrote a short letter to his folks, the first in many a month.

> I believe I can honestly say Pa's investment in me is paying off. I have a couple more thousand in the bank pulling in twelve per cent interest.

He didn't mention the money he had won at poker, for his father was a bit of a martinet and his mother was religious to the extreme.

> Of course I'll never be rich. It's a small ranch with poor rocky soil and I have to buy in the winter hay. But it's a good life and we work hard to improve our lot.
> We're building a waterwheel on the river to grind our own flour, digging a cold store to keep stuff

fresh in summer, and I'm planning to buy a couple of milking goats. Had a bit of trouble with rustlers but hopefully that's the end of it.

My carpentry training has paid off well. Dad would be surprised to see the mortice joints I carved in the pine logs so the cabin walls sit firm and snug. I've put in a bedroom extension as I recently got wed.

Glen paused, dipping his quill pen in the ink, wondering what to say about Katrina. She was not exactly the sort he could introduce to his parents' polite, churchgoing society. So he decided to say no more and ended:

Trust my brothers are behaving themselves and you're both well. Fondest love — Glen.

'What the hell you scratching at?' his wife's voice shrilled to him through the door. 'Come to bed.'

Four candles were burning around the room as she lay on the covers. A bit excessive in his opinion, but he didn't want to say so. Katrina was propped up against the pillow, brushing her hair.

'Believe it or not, I used to have a black gal to do this for me and dress me, fetch and carry.'

'How old were you when the war ended?' he asked as he hoisted off his boots.

'About eleven. But I'm talking about when I was younger. Everything was fine and dandy then, before my daddy went off to be a soldier and got hisself killed. I had a private tutor to learn me my sums and to speak French an' a horrid old witch with icy-cold fingers who taught me pianoforte. I hated it: Mozart, Chopin and that sorta crap.'

Glen smiled at her heresies as he rolled on to the bed beside her. She would often reminisce at nights about Seven Pillars, the big house on the plantation in a town called Jackson,

181

Georgia. Another Jackson, miles away and long ago.

Her mood changed from melancholy to embittered as she spoke about when the Yankees had come.

'They didn't burn us to the ground like they did most others, but there weren't much left, no slaves, no livestock, just an empty shell when they were gone.'

'Did you say you were married?'

'Yes, some carpetbagger turned up demanding unpaid land taxes. My mother was at her wits' end. She had nothing. He turned an eye on me. I was thirteen. 'I could marry the girl in lieu of payment. Say no more,' he said. I was in tears, protesting as they took me off in his trap to Jackson. That red-faced, fat, greedy pig. He rousted up a preacher and wed I was. He dropped my mother back at the house and took me to N'awleans on honeymoon. Wow, that was a wild town. Bands playing. Champagne corks poppin'. We certainly had a time.'

'What happened to your mother?'

'I never saw her again. Heard she went crazy as a loon an' they put her in an asylum.'

'What happened to your husband?'

'He got hisself killed in a saloon brawl. So I teamed up with a handsome gambling man. We worked the riverboats, from N'awleans to St Louis. And back again. He certainly taught me how to play a trick or two among all those fine ladies and gentlemen. Then we got thrown off the boats. Banned from every one. They cottoned on to our cheating ways. So we headed for Kansas City.'

'What happened to him?'

'He got shot, too. Most of my men seem to end up that way. Still, I didn't give a damn. I worked my way through the cattle towns, from Abilene to Dodge City. I was gonna keep going west but somehow I got sidetracked up to Jackson. So here I am in this damn hole. Jackson Hole. Jeez, I got a thirst. Why don't you have some whiskey delivered? Or build your own still like we do down south?'

'Moonshine?' He laughed. 'Firstly, 'cause I'm too busy, secondly I don't need it, an' thirdly because it's illegal.'

'Fourthly 'cause you're too scared to.'

'Come on,' he said. 'Let's get some sleep.'

'Sleep?' She turned, nestling into him, stroking his hair. 'Who goes to bed to sleep?'

★ ★ ★

So spring passed into early summer. White-throated swifts returned to the high cliffs. The sandhill crane's deep, rolling call could be heard again. The sun was warm on their backs as Glen and the two cowboys worked out on the range. Hank's broken leg had mended enough for him to hobble around and help Isaac Newton with his jobs around the homestead.

Even Katrina had been stirred to sweep out the cabin, tidy up, hang out washing, even to scatter corn for the hens. But generally she preferred to sit on the porch and paint her toenails.

On the far side of the river, at the meeting of the three trails, the Jackson Hole Roadhouse had been raised: sturdy log buildings where Zane Hollister, in his fancy waistcoat, now reigned. Beer and whiskey had been freighted in and empty wooden barrels roughly converted to tables and chairs.

Zane leaned on his solid hardwood bar and drawled, 'Nobody told me there'd be so much to setting up a joint like this. We're getting thangs organized, ain't we?'

'Sure.' Kenny was up a ladder nailing their big Confederacy flag on a wall, the blue diagonal cross with stars of the thirteen secessionist states against a blood-red background. 'But where's the customers?'

'They'll be here once we get some good-time gals installed. Why don't you go into Jackson and rustle up a few? The cowboys from the outlying ranches will come running once they get a sniff. And the gamblers, too, to rip off the cowboys. I've ploughed a lot of cash into this place. It cain't fail.'

'What about a band?' Billy Bob said. 'Music, that's what we need.'

'OK. A fiddler, squeezebox player, professor of piano, whoever you can get. Why don't you two go git 'em, an the gals. Promise them the earth. We'll pay 'em peanuts. Here.' He rolled four golden eagles along the bar. 'Buy a covered wagon to bring 'em back in.'

'Yee-hoo!' Billy Bob yelled, as he and Kenny raced to jump on their mustangs.

Zane's predictions were true enough. By midsummer the roadhouse up on its hill beneath Mount Signal was one of the most notorious honky-tonks in West Wyoming. On a clear night, with the wind in the right direction, you could hear the racket and see the lights burning as far off as Glen's side of the river.

'When we gonna pay a visit?' Katrina

wanted to know. 'I'm going crazy stuck in this damned cabin.'

'We ain't.' He was becoming sickened by her laziness and nagging. 'It ain't my sorta place.'

'Oh, listen to li'l Lord Goody-Goody.' It seemed to Katrina, who was afraid of horseback, that the only way she would get there would be on Shanks's pony.

* * *

The next morning Glen decided to ride the black stallion into Jackson.

'Why can't I come?' Katrina moaned.

'Because it takes too long on that old wagon. I've just got some business to attend to at the bank an' some letters to post. I should be back by tonight or early tomorrow.'

He'd only gone ten miles when he realized he'd forgotten the letters.

'Hot damn,' he said, pulling up Amigo. 'We'd better go back and get 'em.'

The cabins were quiet when he returned. The boys had set off to the far side of the range. He guessed Hank and Isaac were busy along mending the split-rail fences they'd put up to keep the marauding elk off their pasture. 'No doubt she's still in bed,' he muttered, but was surprised to see a strange mustang hitched outside.

She was in bed, sure enough. Not alone. When he stepped inside he could hear her moaning and the bedsprings rhythymically groaning. Glen felt as cold and empty as stone, as if all his blood was draining from him. He could hardly believe she would do this to him in his own home. His hand went to the grip of his revolver as he kicked open the bedroom door.

Katrina screamed and Zane spun round, reaching for his southern-make six-gun hanging from a bedknob. He froze when he heard the click of the hammer, then turned and saw the Peacemaker pointed unerringly at him.

'Hey,' he said, spreading his palms.

'Aincha gonna give a man a fair chance?'

'When did you ever give any man a chance?' It was as if there was a voice hammering in his head. 'Kill him. Kill him. Kill him. Kill both of them.'

'Don't be a fool, Glen.' Katrina tried to cover her nakedness and wriggle back away from the firing line. 'What you expect me to do when you leave me alone here all day?'

'You shut up,' Glen hissed, swinging the gun on her.

'Waal.' Hollister tried to force a grin. 'I was only being neighbourly. Come to call on ya. Found her here, askin' fer it. How could I refuse? Us Georgia folk like a get-together now and agin. Ain't doin' you no harm.'

Glen turned the gun back on him and took half-pressure on the trigger, his face tense. Zane's sneer disappeared as he braced himself for the explosion. 'No . . . please . . . '

'Ach! You're not worth it. Either of you. Get your clothes on quick. Get outa my home. Both of you.'

'What?' Katrina squawked. 'You can't do this. It ain't your home. I'm your lawful wife. Wyoming's the first state to give us wimmin the vote. I got equal rights.'

'Get out. She's yours, Hollister. Take her and go. If you can't get her on a horse drag her along the ground behind you. Just get off my property. No, leave your gun. I'll send it to you with all her junk. You can have the damn bed, too. I wouldn't go near it now.'

As Zane, hurriedly, and she, reluctantly, pulled on their clothes, Glen shouted, 'Hurry it up. Get out before I change my mind.'

Out on the porch Katrina stared at him venomously with her cold green eyes.

'I'm going,' she hissed, 'but you ain't heard the last of me, buster.'

'Aw, come on.' Zane grabbed hold of her and slung her bodily over the neck of his mustang. Then he swung himself up into the saddle and spurred away.

'Quit your wailin', woman.'

Glen raised his Colt and sent six bullets whistling after them as he watched them go.

'Good riddance,' he said, with a feeling of great relief. Later, though, when his anger had calmed, a sense of desperate loneliness came over him.

12

'I got the devil in my soul,' Katrina sang out as the horse preacher burst into the roadhouse. 'Ain't no use comin' in here.'

'My journey won't be wasted if there's a tankard of beer to be had.' The curly-haired preacher beamed and planted his fists firmly on the bar. 'I know you're a woman of the world, my dear, so I'm not here to waste words or the Lord's time arguing with you.'

'That's true,' Zane drawled. 'She's past redemption. I can vouch for that. Give this rascal a couple on the house, Katrina, and a bite to eat. We gotta keep in with Him upstairs.'

'To be sure, you seem to be doing well for yourselves,' Repentance remarked, as he swigged his beer. 'I hear you've got a band, too. When do they start? I love a spot of music and dancing, I do.'

'It's too early in the day.' Zane took a drag of his cheroot. 'Come back at midnight.'

'Yes, that'd give you an eye-opener.' Katrina was in her element behind the bar, primped and painted in her low-cut gown. 'All our little prairie nymphs'll be as busy as bunnies by then. Coining it in.'

'Where are the poor creatures?' Repentance Rathbone looked about him at the tables where some unsavoury sorts were lounging around playing cards. 'I'm here to give them absolution for their sins.'

'If thass all you wanna give them, Preacher,' Katrina laughed, 'you'll find them in the shack out the back. They're prettifying themselves in readiness for the night's hard labours.'

'I hear you've been doing some poaching of Mr Murphy's girls. He ain't happy about it.'

'We'll be putting him outa business the way we're going,' Zane declared. 'You tell everybody what a hellhole of sinners this is, Preacher, and you'll be doing us a favour. They'll be coming from far and wide.'

'Dear, dear, what a terrible world it is.' Repentance reached in his buckskin bag for a little bottle. 'I've brought my own holy water. Your neighbours, to be sure, don't like the way you are pollutin' the youth of this fine land. I called in on the Trois Tetons and Cousins ranches this morning.'

'Aha!' Katrina cried, pouring him a whiskey and one for herself. 'Out with it. What did *they* have to say? I *must* hear this.'

* * *

Glen Stone looked up from splitting logs to see a horseman riding across from the river towards him. There was something familiar and yet unfamiliar about the man. He was in a topper and a rust-coloured frock-coat. No, it couldn't be. His brother? Caleb? Yes, it was. A surge of elation rose in him to

194

see his brother again. But at the same time it was undercut by doubt. Whatever it was that Caleb wanted he doubted it would be good.

'Oh, no, not more trouble,' he muttered, as he stood, axe in hand.

'Well, look at you,' Caleb sang out as he drew in the steaming chestnut. 'A regular backwoodsman. You took a bit of finding.' He jumped down and went into a shoulder-slapping, mock-punching routine as if they were still boys.

'So this is it? Your *ranch*?' He looked around at the cabin with hides nailed to the walls, the iron cookpot hanging over a glowing fire in the middle of the yard, the low-hung bunkhouse beneath its stand of pines, the chicken pen, stables and corral. 'I was expecting something grander than this.'

'We've got an oven inside but its easier to prepare meals outside in this sort of weather.' *What am I doing*, he thought, *apologizing to him?* Caleb, so his father had written, had wasted all his patrimony 'in his customary ne'er-do-well way'.

Glen led his brother inside and offered his best chair.

'Made it myself,' he said, proudly. 'And note the pegging of the table. Tight as a drum.'

'Yes, that's what *we* should be. Aren't you gonna offer your brother the drink that cheers after he's come all this way to join you?'

Glen didn't much like the sound of that 'join'. What *was* he here for, apart from a holiday?

'Sorry, I don't drink. Sworn off it.'

'What?' Caleb jumped up and looked in the empty bedroom. 'So, where is she? Your wife?'

'Uh, she's not here. It's a long story.'

'You mean that pretty little thing, your neighbour's daughter you waxed so eloquent about in one of your letters. You mean she's left you?'

'No, not Susan. Another woman. Katrina.'

'She's gone, too? Who are you,

Bluebeard? How many wives you got?' Caleb roared with laughter as Glen started to explain.

'I'm kidding you, kid brother. I know all about it. They told me in Jackson. Why, boy, you're famous — or notorious — all along this valley.'

Caleb tossed off his old town hat and threw his frock-coat on to the bunk. As always, he was attired like a dandy, tight cavalry-twill trews, shiny-backed silk vest, loose cravat. Floppy-haired, good-looking in a boyish sort of way, he had always had a certain charm.

'Well, I never was a ladies' man like you, Caleb. True, I've been a fool. But I'm hoping things might improve.'

'You mean in your love life? I'm beginning to doubt that.'

'Well, we'll see.' Glen got to his feet. 'You'd better rub down that fancy horse of yourn. It still gets chill at nights. I'll put him in a stall. Can't put him in the corral with my stallion. Amigo would kick him to pieces.'

By the time he'd showed Caleb

around Isaac Newton was clanging his frying pan on a swinging horseshoe and yelling, 'Come an' git it.' He doled out game stew on to the men's tin plates and they all crowded into the cabin.

'Good Lord!' Caleb exclaimed. 'This is a free-for-all!' He jostled for room at the table to spoon up his vittles. 'This is a weird and wonderful world you've found yourself, hidden away in these backwoods. Do you know, I could barely understand those people in Jackson, they speak in such a drawl.'

'You should hear the trappers,' Joe hooted. 'Even we cain't understand them.'

'It's a sorta French patois,' Hank explained. 'So how long you here for, Caleb?'

'Oh, I'm here to go into partnership with Glen,' the new arrival replied in his breezy, patronizing way. 'I can see there'll need to be a few changes made around here.'

The men glanced at each other but Glen was so taken aback he was lost for words. By the time he was able to speak Caleb had changed the subject. 'How you boys can go a month cooped up here without any liquor and are only allowed out on pay-day to wet your whistles is beyond me. What do you do to amuse yourselves?'

'We're usually too damn weary by the time we git in from the range,' Jerry remarked. 'We ain't lookin' fer entertainment.'

'Early to bed, early to rise,' Hank drawled. 'That's our way. Most ranchers don't allow their men to booze on their premises. It causes trouble. It don't worry us.'

'Hm, I see.' Caleb looked a trifle put out as Glen poured a tarry liquid from the coffee pot. 'Don't you have cream?'

'I'm gonna get a couple of goats. Those cows are half wild and hell to milk. Don't you want any coffee?'

Joe and Jerry chortled about how buckets had been kicked flying when they tried to do the milking and Caleb grudgingly agreed to have his coffee black. 'Not exactly cordon bleu school of cookery, Mr Newton,' he said, as he picked a bit of meat from a tooth. 'Certainly gamey.'

When the boys yawned and went off to the bunkhouse, Glen said, 'You can sleep on a spare bunk in there.'

'God, no! Much too early. Anyway I'd prefer to sleep in here. You got a deck of cards?'

'No, I'm sworn off them, too. There's only one cot, Caleb. That's mine. You'll have to go on the floor.'

'What? What sort of hospitality is this? Where's all the brotherly love? You seem to forget how I looked after you when you were a young 'un.'

'More like got me into scrapes, as I remember, and blamed me for them. Look, Caleb, I've got to speak frankly with you. It's no use you talking about how you'll reorganize this ranch. It's my ranch and I'm not inviting you to be a partner. Last thing I'd do.'

'What do you mean by that?'

'I mean that I'm happy running it on

my own. We each had two thousand dollars. I've doubled mine and ain't doing too bad. You threw all yours away. Well, that ain't gonna happen here.'

'That's right, blame me for my misfortune. You mean you're not willing to give a helping hand to a chap when he's down?'

'You can have a job as a ranch hand at the same wage as the others, thirty a month. You'll get a fair chance. But if you don't pull your weight . . . ' Glen shrugged, 'you'll have to go.'

'Why, you damned little whipper-snapper! I've a good mind — '

'What? I'm as big and as strong as you now, Caleb. You won't be giving me any more thrashings, I can assure you.'

'Don't be like that. What's got into you? You've got a sullen head on you these days. I can't just be one of the men. You owe it to Ma and Pa. At least make me overseer . . . what do you call it . . . ramrodder? I mean, that old man's had his day. You'll have to sack him. He can hardly climb out of his chair let alone on to a horse. We don't need him.'

'Hank saved my life. When he sold me this spread I offered to take him into partnership but he preferred to just be ramrodder. I'd never have made a go of this place if it weren't for him. As long as I can put food on to the table he stays.'

'Oh, I see why you're so rotten to me,' Caleb retorted, after he had decided to join the others in the bunkhouse after all. 'It's little Miss Goody-Two-Shoes up the road. What's her name, Sweet Sue? Maybe I should take a ride up there tomorrow and introduce myself. Maybe I can sweeten her up for you.'

'You just leave her alone and keep out of my affairs,' Glen shouted, pointing a finger at him.

But Caleb had gone. His parting shot had struck home. It kept Glen on edge, twisting and turning all night.

★　★　★

Susan Cousins wouldn't have been found at her father's ranch the next day, for she was up at 8,000 feet in dry and rarefied air, helping to herd a mob of unruly longhorns up to their high summer pastures. Their way took them through majestic canyons and past jagged peaks silhouetted against a clear blue sky.

'Keep an eye out for that mad cow,' their head man, Collins, warned. 'She's already tossed two of the dogs. She thinks that everybody's intent on separating her from her calf.'

'OK, Ken.' Susan eyed the stomping, bellowing beast, who suddenly rushed them, swinging her spearlike horns at Birdie's belly. The pony leapt aside at the last moment.

Then a bunch of bulls decided to make a break back downhill. Susan and three of the cowboys went after them at a pitched gallop, leaping fallen timber and swerving through boulders and trees, yelling and hallooing until they were racing alongside and could turn them back and up to the main bunch.

The week-long drive was not always as exhilarating, for they tried to go at a more gentle pace so as not to alarm the herd. But, as one of the boys said, 'You never know what these durn critters are gonna do.'

Susan loved the life, even the hardships of winter, when the mercury fell to minus twenty degrees and she had to guard against frostbite if she rode out in the deep snows.

At noon they took a break and she jumped down. She fondled the gentle pony and found her a sugar lump. She looked back at the dark-green swaths of pines and the silver lakes far below. Along to the south was the Trois Tetons spread. An icicle of lonesomeness cut into her at the sight. 'Damn you, Glen,' she whispered, tears clouding her eyes. 'Damn you. Why did you do this to me?'

She wiped her eyes, hitched up her jeans, and leapt back astride the saddle.

'Come on, let's go!'

13

Owls screeched and a fox hurried for the cover of the pines as four shadowy riders encircled the white-faced Herefords. The riders were driving them towards the Snake River, which glimmered beneath the light cast by the silver globe of a full moon.

One of them, Snake Owens, whose hair hung frontier-style down to the shoulders of his tattered macinaw from beneath his battered Stetson, paused to light a quirly as he watched the moaning beeves, cows and calves being herded across the river. He gave a crafty grin and muttered,

'A nice li'l bunch. From him to us. What you could call a good night's work.'

In recent years a lot of hard men and rustlers had been run out of the Kansan cattle towns and Snake was among them. Like others on the lam he had been pushed further and further west, one step ahead of lawmen and vigilantes, until he had finally sought refuge in the remote Jackson Hole region.

Zane Hollister had been glad to employ the murderous back-shooter as one of his fast guns.

★ ★ ★

Glen Stone was saddling his feisty stallion when Joe and Jerry came racing in on their broncos.

'There's a bunch of cows gone from the north range,' Joe hollered.

'What do you mean gone? You sure?' For moments Glen was stunned by the news. 'How many?'

'Near on a hundred. Up by Jenny Lake. We counted 'em yesterday,' Jerry joined in. 'There was five hundred or so. Now there's four hundred. Ain't nowhere they coulda otherwise gone 'cept across the lake an' into the forest. They been rustled, sure enough.'

206

Glen stroked his shaven jaw, deep in thought. Then he strode inside and picked up the Colt revolver he had recently cleaned and oiled. He spun the cylinder with his thumb to check the slugs, then stuck it into his greased holster. He picked up the Winchester and stepped back on to the porch.

'I'm going after 'em,' he gritted out.

But at that moment Sheriff Alison rode into their settlement.

'What's amiss?' he called.

'I've had some cows stole.'

'Where you heading?'

'Zane so-called Green's roadhouse. Where else?'

'Hang on. I'm headin' for that den of iniquity myself. I've had a long ride from Jackson. Gimme a cawfee an' a bite to eat an' I'll jine you.'

*   *   *

From the cover of the pines Kenny watched them ride off and gave them time until they were well away. He picked up a can of kerosene, unscrewed its cap and crawled down towards the back of the cabin.

He's one of them bluebelly soldiers,' he gritted out. 'They burned Columbus to the ground. Zane said so. Burn! Vengeance, it is ourn.'

It so happened that Hank was prowling out back, his rifle in his hands, looking for a rabbit for the pot.

'What'n hell's he doing?' he muttered when he saw Kenny hold the can back in his hands, about to spray it over the dry pine walls.

Hank's immediate response was a fast potshot. *Pow*! The can erupted in flames as the bullet blasted it out of the arsonist's fists. The shock waves of the explosion knocked Kenny back into the bushes. His frock-coat was burning as he rolled away, brushing it down in panic. He leapt to his feet and went bounding away over the rocks as footsure as a deer.

Hank levered the trigger guard to

extract the spent shell and spring-activated a fresh cartridge from the tubular magazine under the barrel into the breech. He hugged the rifle into his shoulder, trying to get a bead on the fleeing figure in the burning coat. Five times he fired but each time the fugitive evaded death by taking a zigzag tack, as if he could feel the sights focusing on to his back.

When he disappeared from sight Hank yelled to the boys to bring wet sacks to beat out the small blaze started by the exploding can.

'That was a narrow one,' he said. 'That li'l rat could've burned us down.'

By then Kenny had reached Black Creek, where he had left his mustang. He dived in the water to douse his smouldering coat. Then he rode off at a double-quick trot.

* * *

'What's that?' the sheriff called out. He turned his mount when he heard the echo of shots bouncing off the mountainside about five miles back along the trail.

'I dunno.' Glen screwed up his eyes and shrugged. 'I guess old Hank's out after some supper.'

'Right, let's go on.' Matt Alison looked up at the new roadhouse on its rise beneath Signal Mountain. 'You ready for action?'

Glen patted his Peacemaker. 'I ain't the fastest gun in the world but it's time we played these rattlesnakes at their own game. On second thoughts maybe my Winchester'll be a better bet. Fifteen bullets is better'n six.'

'Who's this coming?'

'Aw, no,' Glen groaned when he saw Caleb riding down the hill towards them. 'It's my brother. He's supposed to have been helping me on the ranch this past month. Or more like hindering me. Never known anybody do a disappearing trick like he does. Generally in the direction of this joint.'

Caleb hesitated when he saw them,

but then rode the chestnut on towards them. He greeted them in his cheerful way.

'Morning, Glen. Who's your friend?'

For answer the sheriff opened his suit jacket and showed the tin star pinned to his vest.

'Hold it, son,' he said. 'What business you been up to here?'

'What's that got to do with you?' Caleb protested. 'If you must know I've been in an all-night poker game. Is that against the law?'

'I'd like you to accompany us back inside this place. I got a few questions to ask.'

'No, sorry, Sheriff. I've had enough of these backwoods. I'm leaving. Jackson first stop, then Rock Springs to pick up the Pullman to California.' He patted his pocket and smiled. 'Had a bit of luck last night.'

'Maybe.' Matt reached out a hand for the chestnut's reins and turned him around. 'You ain't going nowhere just yet, though. You're comin' along with us. We might need some help.'

It occurred to Glen as they hitched their mounts outside the big cabin that it might be like walking into the lions' den. He had no idea how many men Zane had on his payroll.

'Well, look who's here!' Katrina was behind the long bar, making a start on her favourite tipple, a bottle of brandy, which already seemed to have made her light-headed. 'Lover boy!' She was wearing white kid gloves and her tight turquoise dress plunged deeply fore and aft.

Zane was at one end of the bar, decked out in his check suit. It was early yet, but a few characters who had stayed overnight sprawled around in chairs chatting to a couple of half-dressed girls. Billy Bob was standing behind Zane. Another man whom Glen hadn't seen before, whose dark hair was hanging to his shoulders, turned to give them a baleful regard. He had a hogleg strung to his right thigh; his fingers were flickering towards it.

'Fancy seeing you here, Sheriff,' the horse preacher yelled from his bar stool on the other end of the bar. 'I had no idea you were a drinker.'

'I ain't. But it looks like you are,' the sheriff snapped.

'Just fishing fer souls,' Repentance mumbled, as Matt turned his back on him.

'So, what do you want?' Zane challenged.

'Waal, for a start,' Matt drawled, pointing to the Confederate flag on the wall, 'that's illegal. Incitin' rebellion.'

He strode behind the bar and jerked the flag down. He flicked it across Katrina's head, making her duck, then he trampled it on to the floor.

'That's sacrilege!' Zane shouted.

'Shuddup. Secondly, we're here about a hundred cows stolen from Mr Stone's ranch last night.'

'Yeah,' Glen put in. 'Worth a thousand dollars.'

'A thou'!' Caleb gasped. 'But — '

'Stolen?' Zane shouted. 'What you

mean stolen? I paid that brother of yourn good money fer them cows. Four hundred dollars. He tol' me he was in partnership with you and had authority to sell 'em.'

'What?' Glen turned on Caleb, who had backed away. 'Is that right?'

'Well, I *am* ... ' Caleb blustered, smiling, 'your partner. Or I thought I was. Let's face it. You owe me. Anyway, I gotta be goin'.'

'Stay where you are,' Matt growled. 'You ain't goin'. Not 'til we sort this out.'

'Caleb ain't my partner and I don't owe him nuthin',' Glen said. 'So where are my cows?'

'Aw, on the trail through the Togweetee Pass to the eastern plains by now. I made a nice little profit on 'em. Sold 'em to some fellas I know. How did I know they was stolen?'

Snake Owens had said nothing; he had merely stepped further aside to take a stand away from Zane and Billy Bob. His dark eyes were fixed on them.

'There's one other matter,' Matt told them. 'I asked Murphy what had happened to his roulette table. He said it wasn't his. You'd brought it with you. I see you got it over there.'

'So?' Zane began to look uneasy. He glanced around, straightened up and threw his jacket back, to reveal the Rigdon & Ansley on his hip. 'What's it to you?'

'Waal,' the sheriff drawled, still standing behind the bar beside Katrina. 'One of them cowboys slaughtered over at Idaho Falls survived for a few weeks before he succumbed. He was asked if he remembered anything unusual. All he said was, 'The table. He took the table.' Must admit for a while I couldn't understand what he meant. Until last night when I spoke to Spud Murphy. That was a eureka moment. I knew I got you.'

'Jeez,' Billy Bob whined. 'He knows.'

'Sure do.' Matt spat a gob of tobacco juice their way, as he drew his gun. 'I'm arrestin' y'all charged with the murders and robbery at Idaho Falls. It's no good resisting, boys. Just raise your hands nice and slowly. No false moves. I'm taking you in to see the judge. Then we'll hang you. You, too, Snake, you long-haired freak. I got a Wanted poster on you. Bit of a back-shooter, I hear.'

Striking as fast as the reptile he was named after Snake went for his hogleg. In the blink of an eye he was fanning the hammer, snapping shots at the sheriff as girls screamed and onlookers dived for cover.

Matt Alison ducked down behind the bar. The only damage was to his tall hat, which was cut down to the top of his scalp. Katrina's shrieks added to the commotion as bottles on the shelves were smashed.

The sheriff came up and his better-aimed bullets sent Snake back-pedalling to hit the log wall and slide down, spouting blood.

Zane had joined in the affray, pulling his six-gun out to send an arc of lead from the sheriff to Glen. The young rancher knelt for cover behind a table as slugs whined and ricocheted. He heard a groan and glanced round, to see his brother slumped on the floor.

Zane Hollister had emptied the cylinder of his brass-framed, southern-made pistol.

'Zane!' Katrina shrilled. She sent another gun sliding along the bar to him. But as he reached for it Glen's Colt .44 spat smoke and flame and the big slug bored a hole right through Hollister, sending him spinning. The bank robber's eyes bulged with horror as he hit the floor.

Billy Bob had caught hold of the young girl, Phoebe, and was backing away, using her as a shield. He waggled his revolver.

'Don't shoot or she gets it.'

They were the last words he spoke, for Repentance Rathbone pulled from his buckskin bag a light pocket pistol, a Hopkins & Allen .38 with a three-inch barrel. He extended his arm and his superbly aimed shot took out Billy Bob, leaving a single hole between his agonized eyes.

There was an uncanny silence. Onlookers held their breath and participants carefully looked around as pungent black powder smoke rolled around.

Glen had turned to comfort Caleb, and the sheriff was busy reloading slugs from his pocket, when they were caught off guard.

'What's going on?' Kenny Hayward came through the front door, one hand in the pocket of his worn topcoat. 'You've killed Zane!'

The overcoat pocket erupted as a bullet from the concealed handgun tore through it. The sheriff caught the full force of the bullet in his shoulder. Gasping with pain he collapsed behind he bar.

'You ain't gettin' me, you lousy packrats,' Kenny yelled, swinging around to blaze more bullets through his topcoat at Glen.

'Good for you, Kenny!' Katrina shrieked, bringing a Sharps carbine out from under the bar. She hugged it to her shoulder to take a bead on Glen. He had escaped Kenny's onslaught and had rolled away. Now he came up on one knee, his back to her.

'Kill the Yankee vermin,' she cried.

Repentance Rathbone brought up the .38, calmly squeezed the trigger, and sent Katrina flying into eternity amid her smashed bottles.

The horse preacher turned the .38 on Kenny, but he had backed out of the door, slamming it shut. Repentance and Glen strode over, weapons at the ready, taking care in case he was waiting for them.

'OK,' the rancher hissed. 'Now!'

When they got outside they found that Kenny had performed his usual trick: he had set the hitched horses free before he entered the cabin. That was, apart from his mustang, which he had leapt lithely on to. He could now be seen cross-quirting it fast down the hillside.

Glen darted inside to find his

Winchester, but by the time he got back outside the hardened cut-throat had reached the trail, crossed it, and was heading on to the Cousins's spread.

'Oh, hell!' Glen gasped 'He's going for Susan.'

'You better go catch your horse,' Repentance yelled. 'I'll go see to the sheriff. He looks like he's in a bad way.'

'Do what you can for my brother,' Glen begged him. 'I got no time to lose.'

14

As he cut across the rocky pasture at a diagonal tack to join the trail up to the Cousins's ranch house Kenny Hayward saw a fancy four-wheeled rig turn off the main trail and head up towards him. He spurred his mount and met up with it.

'Where you going, mister?' he called, taking hold of the white mare's reins.

'I'm here to see my fiancée, Miss Cousins.' Randolph Levick was alarmed by the dishevelled appearance of the skinny plug-ugly. 'What was all that gunfire up at the roadhouse? Who are you?'

'Aw, they allus takin' target practice,' Kenny whined, in his deep southern drawl. 'I work here. I'll show ya the way.'

'I can find my own way,' Levick shouted, not at all liking the looks of this fellow. As the mare was released he flicked the whip to set her scooting on and tried to reach for his carbine beneath the wagon seat.

'Hup, girl!'

But before he could whip her into a fast trot Kenny rode his mustang alongside and leapt lightly on to the back of the rig. His wiry forearm, strong as whipcord, wound around beneath the lawyer's chin and tightened its grip.

'What the devil?' was all Levick could choke out as a razor-sharp knife brushed across his throat.

'Doncha struggle, mister. Jest pull that mare in,' Kenny ordered. When Levick grudgingly obeyed, Kenny giggled in his ear.

'Ain't you who gonna have Sexy Sue. It's me. Then guess what ahm gonna do? Ahm gonna cut her up, too.'

He pushed the knife hard, then harder, into Levick's jugular. As blood jetted he kicked him over into the dust.

'Hey, what a nice li'l mare. I think I'll

have her, too. Giddap there.'

He went trotting on up to the big ranch house. It was a still, sunny day and the place appeared to be deserted.

'The men must be out on the range,' he muttered. 'Thass a bit good of fortune. I do believe Lady Luck is with me today.'

Susan Cousins's golden curls were poked out of the house door.

'Hello,' she called. 'Who are you? What are you doing here? Isn't that Mr Levick's surrey?'

'Thass right.' Kenny grinned blackened stubs of broken teeth at her. 'Are ya mammy an' pappy at home? He asked me to deliver a message to y'all.'

'What do you mean? Why should he do that?' Susan stepped out on to the porch as Kenny dug his hand into his burned coat pocket to cock the revolver. 'Where is he?'

'He's up at the roadhouse. He wants to see you.'

'What?' Susan was in her blue jeans and a flowered blouse; her pretty face looked troubled. She did not like the looks of this messenger boy — if that was what he was. The way his fanatic blue eyes stared at her made her feel creepy.

'I can't do that. I'd like you to turn around and go back. Tell him if he wants to see me to come himself.'

'I asked you a question, missy. Is your daddy at home?'

'I . . . ' Susan did not know what to say. Her parents had gone to visit a settler, whose wife was ill, further up the trail. 'Yes,' she lied. 'And the men will be back any minute, too.'

'Is that a fact, sweetheart?' Kenny produced the revolver, pointing it at her. 'You ain't a very good liar, are you? Not that I care 'cause you an' me are gonna have some fun.'

As he stepped down Susan turned towards the door.

'Ain' no use tryin' to run from me. I'll shoot ya iffen you do. Makes no odds to me. I jest kilt your fi-an-cy.'

Susan darted towards the door, her

only way of escape. But he was on to her before she could get in, slamming her face forward against the wooden wall, pressing the cold gun barrel to her temple.

'Waal, ain't that a treat?' He giggled as one grimy hand caressed her buttocks outside the cloth. 'So soft an' sweet an' sexy, eh, Susie?'

Susan didn't reply because she didn't know what to say; her mind was desperate for a plan. But there didn't seem to be one. His hand had ceased its groping down below and was stroking up her bare skin beneath the blouse, closing tightly over her breasts as he gurgled lasciviously in her ear. 'You like that, don' you? You wan' the real thang?' He gripped her tightly by her hair, jerking her head back. 'Right. You gonna git it, baby. Git inside.'

Inside the large two-storey house he looked around and hallooed:

'Anybody home?' He listened. 'No, there don't seem to be. Waal, thass jest fine.'

He carefully laid the revolver aside on a table, tripped her backwards over his knee and slammed her down on to the polished boards.

'Gotcha, ain' I?' he grinned, dribbling with anticipation as he knelt over her and tried to plaster his mouth on hers. 'Thass a good girl. No need to struggle. Now, how d'ya git these damn pants off?'

'You don't.' The girl brought her knee up hard into his groin, flinging him off, spitting away the slime of his kisses. She scrambled upright as he grovelled and groaned.

'Get off me,' she screamed, trying to race to the kitchen to grab a knife. 'Agh!'

Kenny was tougher than he looked. Grimacing as he sprang after her he grabbed her boot and pulled his knife from his scabbard. He dragged her down again, trying to pull her pants down, too.

'Gotcha! he gloated, wriggling up over her and pricking the knife to her throat. 'Now you gonna play fair, or not?'

'Oh, God!' Susan gasped as he ripped her blouse and bodice apart and groped her breasts. Was there nothing she could do? Did she have to let this creature have his filthy way? Her heart was beating fast as he let her sit up.

'Now, git them damn boots off,' he slobbered. 'An' them tight jeans. I don't want no more messin' around.'

He prodded her with the knife as she slowly, reluctantly obeyed his commands.

'Thass better.'

'OK.' She nodded, pulled off one boot and tossed it aside. Then she hauled at the other. 'I'll do as you want. It's a tight fit.'

'Yeah, like you, I bet,' Kenny gurgled, but as he laughed she brought the boot off fast, bashing it into his face. Then she brought it back, to aim the spur at his eyes.

'You hellcat,' Kenny screamed, fending her off, holding her down, such fury in him he could barely prevent himself from slicing the knife across her throat. He pricked her with it, making blood flow. 'I can see I shoulda taken you up into them woods. A good beating is what you need. You just don't know how to be polite.'

Susan glared at him and when he tried to kiss her again bit his lip hard.

'Bitch!' he hollered, jumping back. 'You're askin' for it now.'

★ ★ ★

Amigo was in two minds whether to make a break for freedom and the wilds, where he could gallop back and forth, or to return to the man who at least didn't whip and spur him like others had before him, and who usually had a tasty cracker in his pocket. At last Glen's whistle to him won the day and he trotted hopefully back. Glen stuck the Winchester into the boot and jumped on to his back.

'Come on, boy,' he cried. 'Go!'

He slowed his mad gallop to the Cousins's place only when he found Levick's corpse on the trail; then he cantered on. He halted before he reached the buildings, sensing the air like an animal: a predator. He slipped from Amigo and went forward on foot, the Winchester in his grasp.

He burst through the door and saw Susan sprawled almost naked on the floor.

'Watch out!' she shrieked.

Glen half-looked up to see a knife flashing towards him. It sliced across his shoulder as he smashed it away with the Winchester, to go clattering into a corner. There was pain and blood and the rifle in his hands wavered.

The demented Kenny punched him to the floor and leapt over the two of them to grab his long-barrelled Lefaucheux from the table. He grinned evilly and fired. The slug hit the Winchester's frame and knocked it from Glen's hands.

He and Susan froze as the killer

raised his revolver to fire again. But when Kenny squeezed the trigger there was an ominous click. He was either out of lead or the pistol had jammed.

'Hell take it!' Kenny gave a scream of fury, hurled the pistol at them, then pulled another slim, razor-sharp knife from his boot. 'This ain't the end.' He grinned. 'Or it is for you.' He leaped on to the rancher.

From then on it was a trial of strength as Kenny went into the attack, stabbing with the knife. Glen caught his wrist with his good hand, At first the knife came hard towards his chest, then he held it at bay, gritting his teeth with the effort. Kenny seemed possessed by a satanic strength.

Susan backed away, watching the two men in their battle as she slid across the floor. She struggled to her feet and staggered towards the kitchen.

Her heart pounded as she found the Smith & Wesson in a drawer. Her hands were shaking so that she could hardly pick up the bullets to push into the cylinder. She took a deep breath and calmed herself.

'Right,' she said.

The two men were still struggling when she went back. Suddenly Glen saw her, standing half-naked, the revolver gripped in both hands, her blue eyes staring as she tried to aim at Kenny. Glen knew he needed to get out of the line of fire. He hurled the man away and rolled aside.

'Hold it right there,' Susan cried. 'You varmint!'

Kenny turned and gave a quivery smile, raising the blade to hurl it at her. Susan couldn't hesitate. She fired. The .44 slug smashed through the outlaw's chest, blasting his heart apart.

Susan kept on firing as he jerked and twisted in agonized spasms, until the cylinder was almost empty. 'You . . . you filth! You slime! How dare you?'

She shook her head with dismay. 'I've killed him,' she sobbed.

'You had to,' said Glen. 'He would have killed you.'

'Yes.' She stared strangely at Glen on the floor, the smoking gun in her hands. 'I guess you saved my life. I couldn't have fought him off much longer. Then I saved yours.'

'So,' he ventured, 'perhaps we're quits. Friends again?'

'*You!*' She fell on top of him, sobbing and shaking. She tossed the gun away and, as it exploded its last shot, she found his lips. 'Why do you do this to me?'

Glen hugged her into his arms, kissing her like he'd never kissed a woman before, soothing her, stroking her bare body as if he could hardly believe this was true.

'I guess that means yes.' He smiled at her and winced as he struggled up on one elbow and took a look at his cut. 'We're both lucky to be alive.'

'Are you OK?'

'I'll survive.' He tenderly touched the prick of blood on her neck. 'How about you?'

'Never felt better.'

'Seems like we're two of a kind. Maybe,' he muttered, 'we oughta clear up the mess and these bodies 'fore your parents get home.'

'Aw, we've plenty of time,' she whispered, snuggling into him, seeking his lips again. 'All the time in the world.'

★　★　★

Three months had passed. The sheriff had recuperated well. Susan's parents had put in a hundred-dollar bid for the roadhouse when it was put up for public auction and now ran it as a respectable hotel. Caleb had sent a postcard from California and it sounded as if he had, as always, landed on his feet. Repentance Rathbone, an agent working undercover for Wells Fargo, had recovered most of the stolen cash. He had found it stuffed into the mattress of Katrina and Zane's big bed. While Hank ran the southern range Glen and Susan had moved into the ranch house on the northern range after their wedding. To save young Phoebe from a life of sin they had taken her as their hired domestic help. All was going well.

Today they had set off on a delayed honeymoon, riding Amigo and Birdie, with Crackers as the pack-horse. They had paused a while by the two graves marked with simple wooden crosses on a flower-covered bank of the river.

'Katrina wasn't a bad woman,' he said. 'I suppose she was just kinda wild.'

'Randy was an odd one, too,' Susan remarked.

'They were both too young to die.'

They rode on northwards, planning to join the crowd waiting to see President Arthur, who was, himself, riding 350 miles, hunting and shooting buffalo along the way, to view the wonders of the Yellowstone.

The aspens on the banks of the zigzagging Snake were magnificent in the golden colour of fall, and the clear sunshine illumined the other snow-capped peaks, all of them over 10,000 feet, in the Teton range to the north-west: the Thor, the Rolling Thunder, the Eagle's Nest and others in the dramatic panorama.

'Oh! I felt our baby's first kick.' Susan's eyes sparkled as she reached out a hand to his. 'This is just the start of things for us.'

'Yeah,' Glen replied, as he listened to moose bugling up in the dark green forest. 'We got a lifetime ahead.'

We do hope that you have enjoyed reading this large print book.

Did you know that all of our titles are available for purchase?

We publish a wide range of high quality large print books including:
**Romances, Mysteries, Classics
General Fiction
Non Fiction and Westerns**

Special interest titles available in large print are:
**The Little Oxford Dictionary
Music Book, Song Book
Hymn Book, Service Book**

Also available from us courtesy of Oxford University Press:
**Young Readers' Dictionary
(large print edition)
Young Readers' Thesaurus
(large print edition)**

For further information or a free brochure, please contact us at:
**Ulverscroft Large Print Books Ltd.,
The Green, Bradgate Road, Anstey,
Leicester, LE7 7FU, England.
Tel:** (00 44) **0116 236 4325
Fax:** (00 44) **0116 234 0205**

Jason Brand's latest assignment takes him into the mountains, searching for two missing men — a Deputy US Marshal and a government geologist. But this apparently routine assignment turns out to be anything but. For Bodie the Stalker, hunting a brutal killer, rides the same trail. It's just another manhunt for him — until he finds himself on the wrong end of the chase. But then Bodie meets Brand. And when they join forces, it's as if Hell itself has come to the high country . . .

GUNS OF THE BRASADA

Neil Hunter

Ballard and McCall are in Texas, working for Henry Conway, an old friend, on the Lazy-C ranch. But trouble is brewing: Yancey Merrick, owner of the big Diamond-M, kept pushing to expand his empire. Then Henry's son Harry is run down through the brasada thicket before being shot in the back and killed. Determined to find the guilty party, Ballard and McCall suddenly find themselves deep in a developing range war . . .

LONELY RIDER

Steve Hayes

He calls himself 'Melody', after the word burned inside his belt. Because he can't remember his own name — or anything at all prior to the past six weeks. It's 'amnesia', according to Regan Avery, the woman he rescues from a fast-flowing river. But Melody doesn't need the fancy name for his predicament to know he's in trouble — for the few things he *can* remember involve being shot at and wounded, with a posse hard on his heels . . .

GILA MONSTER

Colin Bainbridge

A stagecoach is on its way to the small town of Medicine Bend when it is attacked by outlaws. However, the coach's passengers manage to repel them. This disparate array of characters — the new marshal Wade Calvin; Mr Taber, insurance salesman; and Miss Jowett, on her way to take on caring for her widowed nephew's children — thus find their lives intertwined. But as they settle into life in Medicine Bend, Gila Goad, the outlaws' vicious leader, hears news of the botched robbery — and is determined to get his revenge . . .

THE GUN MASTER

Rory Black

On his way to visit an old friend, Rex Carey arrives in the township of Willow Creek. But, unbeknownst to him, the infamous Zane Black is is staying in the same hotel. Soon Rex, known throughout the West as the Gun Master, clashes with Zane, and blood is spilled. Meanwhile, Forrest Black is riding towards Willow Creek with his men, with no idea he is about to find his brother Zane dead. Determined to avenge him, Forrest and his outlaw gang are on a collision course with Rex . . .

SHOT TO HELL

Scott Connor

Bounty hunter Jarrett Wade gained his fierce reputation when he defeated the bandit Orlando Pyle in Hamilton. But, several years on, Wade has lost his edge, and is reduced to taking any lowly assignment he can find. A chance to regain his past glory appears when he's offered an apparently simple assignment. He readily accepts — but before he can complete the task, he's gunned down and left for dead . . .